Roxanna Cross

SIZZLING
TEASERS

Published worldwide in 2014 by

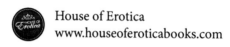

House of Erotica
www.houseoferoticabooks.com

An imprint of Andrews UK Limited
The Hat Factory
Bute Street
Luton, LU1 2EY

Contents

This book is dedicated first and foremost to my family. Without their loving support and understanding this work would have never seen the light of day. A special thank you goes out to my parents who have taught me never to give up on my dreams as they are now baring fruits. And to my husband and girls all I can say is…sorry I live in my own head so often. I do appreciate that when I come of my bubble you are all there for me. I love you guys.

SIZZLING
TEASERS

Strangers in the Night

While waiting for an answer on the other side of the line, Jay cradled the phone in the nook of his neck and shoulder.

With a sigh he dropped the phone on the soft golden duvet. He racked his hair with unsteady hands. Thoughts of home overwhelmed him. *Could it be that in the few weeks spent on the road...* Jay stopped the thought before it could fully formulate. The essence of it made his insides coil. *Why no answer?*

His gaze settled on the red digits of the clock radio 10:57. Later than usual, yet he couldn't bring himself to stretch out and fall asleep. They always talked before falling asleep, a special rule of theirs – one he cherished.

His lips curved into a smile as he remembered waking up with the phone glued to his face a couple days ago. The smile quickly faded as he pictured the phone ringing unanswered on the bedside table in the master bedroom. Then the image of the empty king sized bed flashed across his mind. *Or maybe it's not empty.* His thoughts twisted in fury. He shook his head to erase the painful picture.

Pinching his lips together, he jerked his arms out of the long white cotton sleeves of the bathrobe and tossed it roughly on the bed. "Sonofabitch," he cursed when his watch caught on a loose thread. Jay yanked on the offending piece of fabric, then pulled on his jeans and sweater before leaving the room.

***

Savannah wiped down the tables and picked up the empty plates with robotic movements. Her mind drifted far away from the 5th Street Soda Shoppe where she worked seven days a week. She just couldn't shake the unnerving thoughts.

Honestly girl, fretting over a crazy gypsy fortune teller's reading! It's all nonsense, she told herself. *The old lady just made it all up. Its way too twisted to be true. I would never. I would never. I would never.* She repeated this mantra to herself to keep some form of sanity. Unfortunately, it didn't help. Savannah cursed her own stupidity – letting words, absurd ones at that, stress her out.

Dammit!

Why couldn't she shake them? Engrossed in her circling thoughts, she moved around the Shoppe like a robot, not paying attention to any of the patrons. Arms loaded with dirty dishes, she backed out of the last red vinyl booth seat, tucked away in a far off corner, and slammed right into a hard surface. The crash of dishes bounced off the thin walls and made her ears ring.

When the hell did we put in a wall here?

She hated bending over in this 50s-era flippy waitress skirt that the owner called a uniform.

Why did I ever take this stupid job?

Dozens of reasons swarmed around her mind. Primarily, the fact that her ex-fiancé had cleaned out their joint bank account and disappeared off the face of the earth with their entire life savings – a small fortune – but one she needed all the same. That jerk had wined her, dined her, bedded her, and given her the most exquisite ring, and then *wham*! Three months before the wedding, he'd vanished – the bastard – leaving her with all the wedding debts and piles of credit card bills, not to mention the mortgage on the brand-spanking-new condo they'd just bought – which she hadn't been able to sell.

Waitressing had become the best way to make the extra money she so desperately needed to keep a roof over her head.

Resigned, she bent over and pulled her left knee onto the squeaky vinyl seat, giving herself extra leverage to reach under the table. She hated to have her butt exposed for all to see, but the dishes certainly weren't going to pick themselves up.

***

Jay walked into the Soda Shoppe and ordered a malt chocolate shake. He appreciated the authentic feel of the little diner: the black and white ceramic tiles, chrome counters, chequered tablecloths, red vinyl stools and booths, and the old fashioned mixers along the back wall. A cosy haven for lost treasures of the 50s.

With his eyes locked on the various memorabilia on the walls, he made his way to the far corner booth. Suddenly, a tall slender figure bumped into him. It took him a few seconds to realize that his shake had dripped all over him. The ice cream seeped through the cotton of his shirt and he didn't care. The heat infusing him from within counteracted the icy mess. As if in a trance, he wiped it away and placed the half-empty glass on the table top.

He couldn't keep his eyes off the long shapely legs and curvy buttocks in front of him. He wanted to clear his throat and apologize. Instead, he swallowed hard when the buttocks made contact with his loins. His cock sprang to life and pulsed uncomfortably against the tight confines of the denim. Without thinking, he reached out to caress the lovely cheeks. Blinking rapidly and licking his now very dry upper lip, he stopped himself when his fingers were mere inches away from the elevated bottom.

What the hell is happening to me?

***

Savannah felt instant heat in her lower abdomen when her buttocks grazed the bulging head of a hard cock.

Not a wall. A man. I backed into a man. And now my butt is perfectly aligned with his cock.

Savannah knew that she should stand up right away. She should pull forward – move away from the heat.

She didn't.

She looked down and saw the broken pieces of the last plate under the table. To bend down lower would be *very naughty.* She bit her lip.

When's the last time you've been naughty? Never, that's when. Grab this opportunity now!

Ignoring her logical brain, she acted on impulse and bent down lower.

Lower.

Until she knew that the stranger behind her would get an eyeful of her hot pink G-string.

***

Jay held his breath.

Seconds ticked by; his heart slammed against his chest as if keeping time. Still she remained stock still. Sweat beaded on his forehead. His jaw automatically locked as he gritted his teeth together and silently prayed. *Please straighten up. I beg you to move away from my raging hard-on. I can't...*

Heat consumed him when he watched her body bend lower. The beads of sweat trickled down his spine as he fought to bottle up the wild lust surging through him. Lust he couldn't phantom to understand because he hadn't felt it rise inside him for years. Confusion with a hint of despair clouded his brain. Confused or not, he lost the battle when the beautiful buttocks made second contact and he caught a glimpse of the hot pink string wedged between the *oh-so tempting* flesh. When his fingers twitched forward he didn't stop them. This time he let his hands roam free. His fingers glided over the soft skin and slowly made their way to the tiny string.

She'll pull away. She'll stand up, slap me the face. Fuck, she has to do something to stop me. No, I need to stop myself. Shit, I shouldn't be doing this.

Even though his thoughts screamed at him to stop, his fingers kept trailing downwards; slowly he reached under the soft string and pushed it aside.

***

Savannah's heart raced.

A stranger invaded her personal space – strong hands touched her body – and by God, she liked it!

Moisture pooled between her pussy lips when his fingers reached under the string of her underwear. She wanted, no, she craved his fingers slipping inside her. She needed to feel his thumb circle her clitoris.

To be honest, she really wanted his hard cock pumping inside of her, wild and fast, hard and slow. She moaned deep inside her throat when his fingers trailed along her juicy slit.

***

Jay felt like a firecracker – all lit up and ready to explode. Every breath he took filled him with more heat – heat that fuelled his desire for this beautiful stranger bent before him. He shifted to readjust the torturous pressure of his erection against his fly. He wanted to release it and drive it deep inside of her – to feel her juices flow over his tight, hyper-sensitive skin.

He heard a moan of desire escape her, and couldn't believe it. The sweet sound of her voice ringing in his ears broke the last of his restraint. His hands shook as he let them travel between her legs and caressed the soft thatch of curls hidden there. Another moan floated out of her. With his thumb, he circled her throbbing clitoris.

Oh holy shit, she wants this just as much as I do. And the fact that he did want *her terrified him. He couldn't help it the fire surged through him and it couldn't be denied.*

Even though he know he would have to dive in his twisted psyche later, he stayed in the here and now and let his out-of-control-body take over. With his free hand, he reached under her T-shirt and glided his fingers along her well-toned body. He cupped her left breast and felt her nipple harden through the thin lace of her bra. He wanted to feel the silkiness of her skin in the palm of his hand, so he found the little clasp between her heaving breasts. In one quick motion he flicked the bra open and felt the grapefruit sized breasts come spilling out.

***

Savannah tingled with desire. Every inch of her felt alive, wired and electrified. His touch sent sparks of pure lust to her sex. Her body sang under his caresses – completely in tune to this stranger behind her.

She felt his hand tremble when he ran his fingers into her tiny curls. That little tremble, that small show of him losing control, moved her. She wanted to feel his touch everywhere on her body.

He did not disappoint her. With his free hand, he reached under her T-shirt and traced her rib cage. She recited a little prayer of thanks to the God-of-broken-down-appliances, because with her washer on the fritz, she'd been left with no choice but to wear her front-clasping bra that morning.

He flicked it open and her aching nipples fell into his warm soft hand.

In a bold movement, Savannah snaked her arm behind her body and let her fingers trail the length of him. His erection seemed to go on forever – what a dream come true! He groaned out loud when her fingers reached his zipper tab. She almost lost hold of it when his index finger slipped inside of her.

In slow motion his finger continued to rock in and out of her tight wet folds. All the while, his thumb strummed her clitoris in quick little flicks. Blood rushed in her ears as her pulse quickened. Her thighs trembled. The moisture between her pussy lips kept building and building.

***

The moment her delicate hand touched his pants, Jay thought he would explode and pour a cupful of semen into his boxers.

He wanted inside of her, *now!*

He moved his finger with ease in and out, in and out. When her muscles clenched around his knuckle he wanted so much to feel those same muscles tighten around his erect cock.

Fuck, this feels good. Too good! What the hell is wrong with me?

Jay couldn't wrap his mind around the events that were unfolding... when his zipper went down and slim fingers fumbled to unbutton his boxers, all thoughts left him. Nails scratched his engorged head and trailed down to the base of his cock. The small hand wrapped around his thick shaft and pumped once, twice, and droplets of semen spat out of his pulsing purple head. He took his hand out of her T-shirt and gently grabbed her wrist.

The pumping motion stopped.

***

Savannah stayed motionless, holding her breath.

She didn't want him to pull away from her and whimpered in complaint when his index finger slipped out of her. With strong hands, he grabbed her waist and his long fingers dug into her flesh – a little thrill shot through her.

Her vaginal muscles pulsed with anticipation.

***

Jay drove his thick cock deep inside of her. In one swift motion he pulled out and plunged back inside. Again and again, he pulsed forward and back and forward again. His hold on her waist grew stronger and stronger as the blood rushed to his leaping cock. He knew there would be bruises on the delicate skin under his palms and he wanted to release his hold – he just couldn't. He kept thrusting in and out of her furiously.

Her pelvis ground into each of his wild plunges, driving his cock deeper inside – so deep he didn't know where he ended and she began. He'd never felt so enveloped before. Tight, hot and wet walls squeezed him all around – maddening how unbelievably tight she held him. With her growing hotter, wetter, *and oh holy shit*, tighter, around his engorged cock, he knew he wouldn't last much longer.

Jay wanted, *needed*, her to climax as well. He released his hold on her hips, and dipped his hand downwards. With his thumb and index finger, he teased and pinched her swollen clitoris. He slammed his pelvis forward, driving his cock so deep that for a second he thought he would rip her open. That thought almost made him stop cold. Her muscles clenched his cock in quick succeeding motions. Her hips, her ass, her thighs bucked against him.

She groaned. The sound of her pleasure electrified his senses – sent his heart rate into overdrive. His lungs worked double-time to pull in whatever air he could manage to gulp. His entire body shook from the effort he exerted, pummelling her sweet pussy into the ecstasy she richly deserved. When her creamy juices poured over him, sliding the length of his cock, he came undone. Blinded by an uncontrollable need to empty himself, he pumped, hard, fast and wild, reaching deeper and deeper within.

**

Savannah felt a second orgasm build. How could she not? His huge cock stretched her to the limit, reaching that border line of sweet pain when he drove into her with almost brutal force. She rocked her ass backwards, bringing him farther in. His engorged head expanded – expanded so much it nudged that *oh-so difficult to find* G-spot. She wanted more of him *there* – all of him there. She thrust backwards, impaling herself on his length, making him slam on that precious spot.

"Yes, yes. More. God, give me more," she screamed – out loud or in her head, she couldn't tell.

It must have been out loud because she received more.

His cock plunged inside of her with animalistic need – primal, raw, exclusive. That need drove them both over the edge.

Her muscles constricted hard and fast, squeezing his cock tighter and tighter around her wet heat. She felt his body tremble with the force of his orgasm. Hot liquid filled her – his, hers, blended together into a thick cream that caressed her sensitive inner walls.

**

A clatter at the door pulled the strangers out of their sexual bubble.

They both whipped around, a little stunned to find themselves in a public diner.

Jay quickly pulled out of the warm confines of the stranger's vagina and stood there dripping in her juices, eyes locked with the patron at the door.

"The concierge at the Hotel said I might find you here."

The hurt in Damon's soft voice filled Jay with guilt. He zipped up and ran after the retreating figure.

"Damon, wait. Please, Damon. Let me explain."

Damon didn't stop. He kept walking away. Something inside of Jay ripped open and nearly sent him to his knees. Only the acute awareness that he inflicted this bleeding pain onto... Well, now he knew how it felt like to break a man and his feet started running.

***

Savannah's body jerked with erotic aftershocks.

As her mind reeled, her brain unable to catch up with the flow of emotions, Savannah mechanically straightened herself out of her contortionist's position. She didn't even know how long her mind-blowing encounter had lasted. She only knew that the sexual spell had broken the moment the Matthew McCaughey look-alike walked into the Soda Shoppe.

Did this really happen?

The small drops of cum sliding down her thighs proved it. She didn't see her mysterious lover – only glimpsed his long, muscled legs in tight denim running out the door after the man who'd pulled them from their fantasy...?

Savannah didn't even bother picking up the discarded dishes. She simply untied her apron, threw it across the booth and, with sure and steady steps, walked out of the Soda Shoppe.

Midnight Snack

At two in the morning I heard silence in the house. Unable to sleep I padded into the kitchen of my employer's home, and opened the fridge, which I hadn't cleaned out earlier like I should have. Quickly, I started pulling out the leftover containers and re-organizing the fruits and vegetables. In the midst of wiping down the last shelf my employer sneaked up on me.

"Nina, what are you doing up so late?"

The bottle of water in my hands clattered on the glass shelf. I whirled around.

"Mr. Beck, you scared me."

"I'm sorry Nina. I didn't expect you to be up and about this time of night."

From the towel loosely wrapped around his waist and naked torso I could tell he really hadn't expected to find me in the kitchen.

"Did you have trouble putting Andrew down?"

"A little," I confessed, "but he calmed quickly enough when I starting singing to him. He's been asleep for hours now. I just couldn't sleep," I finished lamely.

He arched his eye brow and said, "So you decided to clean out the fridge at two in the morning." A smile played on his lips.

"I guess so." My voice quaked a little. Never before in all my twenty-one years had I been so up close and personal with the opposite sex. For a man in his thirties, Kristopher Beck equalled *hot, hot, hot.*

Six feet three inches of knotted muscles and tanned skin. Sandy brown hair and eyes as clear as the sky, not to mention perfect white teeth beaming with each smile. No wonder my heart still raced. His washboard abs displayed perfectly above the loose knot of the white cotton towel, which stopped in the middle of his precision cut quadriceps. Water droplets shone on his skin. My body grew hot. My breath felt heavy in my lungs, and my nipples hardened against the build-in bra of my spaghetti strap tank top as my cheeks flushed pink. *God, I hope he didn't see that.* I turned my body inside the fridge and pulled out some ham and rye bread.

"Can I fix you something to eat?" I gulped out.

Kristopher stepped closer to me and reached for the loaf of bread and container of ham. He deftly took them from my hands and dropped them on the counter. His body mere inches away from mine, I could smell the soap and shampoo on him, like spring rain renewing the fresh earthy tones. The minty toothpaste on his breath made my mouth water.

"Nina, if I were to tell you that the only thing I am hungry for is you, how would that make you feel?" His voice, low and husky, played havoc on my senses and left me breathless – voiceless. I felt my eyes grow large and round. My nostrils flared. My body trembled.

"Has a man ever tasted you here?" He asked in a husky whisper.

I still felt the burn of his fingers where they glided down my tank strap to get where they are now; circling my lengthened nipple. Quicksilver ran in my veins. I shook my head from side to side, answering him – NO. The sweet burn of his fingers spread lower as they skimmed my rib cage, and dipped down past my belly button.

"How about here?" He rasped as his fingers cupped my mound.

The air left my lungs. Bubbles of lava spurted to life in my lower abdomen. This time my muscles wouldn't cooperate I couldn't even shake my head no. I lost myself in the feeling of his fingers flicking my clit through the thin material of my pajama bottoms. He raised his other hand so close to my breast – but reached past me to open the freezer compartment. Baffled, I stayed paralyzed in the bliss his fingers provided *down there.*

His hand never left my mound as he unwrapped one of Andrew's lime Popsicle treats with the long deft fingers of his other hand. My mind raced at the possibilities as my heart slammed against my rib cage. I watched in rapt attention as his full sensual lips closed over the tasty pop – finding something primal in the act. When he released the Popsicle and held it up in the air, eyes focused intensely on me, my heart stopped.

"You are so beautiful Nina and I've wanted for you for so long," he said before bending his head down and claiming my lips. They tasted of lime and man. God, I have never tasted anything better! I felt an explosion inside of me – like a flood building behind a gateway. My breathing grew rapid and heavy. Every cell in my body ignited with the force of the eruption that I felt coursing through me, full speed ahead.

He traced the length of my throat with the cold sticky treat and I gladly exposed it to him; it felt so natural for my head to fall back... I craved his touch that much. An icy shiver ran through me. Goosebumps formed under my skin. My limbs began to quake. *Oh my, this is... so erotic.* The lime Popsicle kept trailing down further between my cleavage. I didn't care about becoming sticky, or that my top would stain from where the Popsicle now circled. I felt on fire for this man, whose one hand massaged my covered pussy while the other branded me with an icy treat.

The fire only raged more when his mouth followed the sticky trail: licking, sucking my lime-slick skin. My back arched, pushing my breasts towards the eagerly searching mouth. He took the hint and popped one silk covered nipple between his lips. Even through the thin material the sensation of his hot breath and hotter tongue felt incredible – relieving the tiny prickles of the icy pain. His fingers travelled up my arms and slipped under the straps. He pulled them down, exposing the top of my creamy breast and peachy nipple. He circled me with the ice again, making me shiver all over, then his mouth released the clothed nipple and captured the naked one – suckling the lime juice off my body.

He left me in awe of him as his other hand never stopped the delicious ministration to my mound. My legs shook from an incomprehensible need to... let go. Everything inside tightened and coiled.

Ecstasy! The flood poured out of me and soaked my pajama bottoms.

"God, Nina, you are so responsive to my touch. This is such a turn-on to see you like this. Puffy lips, puffier nipples, wet cunt. The smell of your sex." He took a second to breathe deeply. "Rich sweet musk is intoxicating. I want to taste it."

He looked at me with a wicked smile as he reached across the counter and pulled the jar of honey forward. With the glass container in the crook of his elbow, he dropped to his knees, pulled down my baggy bottoms and exposed my juice-slicked lips. "So beautiful," he said, as he twisted the jar open. He took out the honey droplet and dabbed it on my clit and slit before starting to lick my labia. "So tasty, such sweetness," he purred and continued to lap up my oozing cream mixed with the honey.

His tongue pushed my inner lips open and dipped inside for only a moment, then he inserted the covered honey droplet, coating my inner walls with the thick sweetener. My fingers dug into his hair. The Popsicle still circled my nipples. The honey droplet stretched my pussy. My heart pounded to a rhythm unknown to me. Kristopher revelled in making me his, enjoying the way my body reacted to each new sensation. His tongue traveled from my nipples to my navel and my public bones getting closer and closer to my honey-dripping pussy.

Kristopher took the Popsicle into his mouth, now melted to a stub, and left a trail of sloppy, sticky, open-mouthed kisses down my sternum, dipping into my navel, licking my lower abdomen, dabbing my honeyed clit. Oh, the icy treat on my flaming button made my pelvis rotate. I opened my thighs wider – an act of utter wantonness – a fact he didn't ignore. He took advantage of this extra room, settling his broad shoulders under my thighs.

Deftly his fingers twisted the honey droplet out of my pink folds. The glass instrument clattered to the floor as he buried his face in my pussy, tongue deep inside – pushing the last of the Popsicle in my wet heat. The contrast overwhelmed me.

"Ohhhhhhhh," a long throaty moan escaped my trembling lips. My hips bucked on his face as his tongue went in deeper – licking my lime-honey-slick inner walls, twirling my juices round and round and swallowing. His lips found my hard swollen clit and latched at it – sucking it deep. I pulled on his hair and pushed his face farther inside my open pussy lips. My pelvis tilted forward at the same time, giving him more of me to lick and suck and slurp.

He didn't disappoint me. His tongue worked like a branding iron, claiming me as his. His fingers moved slowly up and down my lips and found my entrance; one slipped inside, he moved it slowly in and out. His tongue flicked my clit as my hips undulated, gyrating to a primal rhythm, and I felt the surge of lava coursing though me again. I bucked and thrashed against him as the flood came like white rapids cresting, peaking, *oh God*. I came hard and fast on his tongue and finger.

He licked me clean and sucked in his finger to clean it off as well. When he pulled himself up from between my legs, his towel and honey jar remained forgotten on the floor.

"Nina, I want you." He cupped my face in his hands and kissed me. He tasted of honey and lime and me; the mix –

intoxicating. He poured such tenderness into this kiss it made my heart swell.

I felt brave enough to admit what I'd known for quite some time. "Kristopher..." I searched his eyes. In nearly two years of working for this man, I'd never before used his given name.

His eyes shone when I said it.

"Kristopher," I said again, "I want you, too."

As if the words released something inside of him, like they were all he needed to hear, he crushed his lips to mine. His hands skimmed down my spine, squeezed my ass and lifted me up. He didn't need to tell me he'd be gentle. His slow sensuous movements and sensitive touch on my skin told me everything I needed to know. His kiss remained soft and tender as he lowered me down onto his erection: kissing me, massaging my breasts, teasing my clitoris as he pushed me down.

When his bulbous head pierced my hymen, my body stiffened in his embrace. He deepened our kiss, played with my nipples and clit until I relaxed again.

"God, Nina, you feel so good, hot, wet and so incredibly tight. I want to ride you like this forever." He groaned as his cock moved languidly in and out of my juicy folds. He kissed my lips, my chin, my throat, the vein erratically pulsing under my earlobe, which made my muscles constrict around his girth.

"That's it baby. Squeeze me tighter, damn that feels good." The vibration of his voice against my hammering pulse drove me wild, and in quick succeeding motions my muscles squeezed and squeezed.

He pumped inside of me faster, slapping his balls against my ass as he reached deeper inside of me with each savage thrust. I felt my blood turn into fiery sludge. The oxygen in my lungs grew heavy. My stomach knotted and exploded. White fire raged through me. I arched my back, slammed my hips down on his upward thrusts and clamped my muscles around his erection, milking him to the last drop. Hot thick cream – mine, his – oozed out of my overfilled pussy.

His lips claimed mine in another slow tender kiss. His fingers dipped in my long curls. We broke apart, breathless. "I've wanted you for so long. I can't let you go now that I've tasted you." He searched my face.

"Kristopher, I've wanted you for so long as well, I have been afraid to let you know. I didn't want to overstep. I know you loved Claire and I didn't want to take her memory away from you."

"Oh Nina, Claire will always be a part of me. She's given me Andrew." His normally sky blue eyes turned dark and murky as he spoke, "Things were extremely rough after her death. When you came to live with us... it got better. You were able to give Andrew what I couldn't through my grief. Now I am able to enjoy the time I spend with my son." His voice trailed off.

I leaned forward and kissed him.

The gloom dissipated from his eyes when we pulled apart.

"Kristopher, can this work?" I hoped I hadn't misread his intentions.

My question hung in the air for a moment or two as if is brain processed all the possibilities: our age difference for one and the fact that he is my employer for another. His lips came down on mine.

"Nina," he murmured. "You need to be honest with me."

His lips felt like soft velvet brushing over mine I needed to remind myself to breathe and respond.

"Mmmmm-mmmmm always."

"Does my age bother you?"

"Not a lick." I answered honestly.

His lips curved in smile as they came down on mine once again.

"That's fantastic," he whispered. "Oh, and Nina, you're fired. I can't have my future wife working for me. Now I am taking you to bed. I want to make love to you again."

I smiled and squeezed his hardening cock in response.

Meet & Greet

She taps on the door, her heart races to a highland tattoo she can't control – she's never done this before. *What am I doing here?* The thoughts echo in her mind as she stands in the empty corridor on the top floor of the Four Points Sheraton Hotel. No time to reflect on her racy decision now...

The Suite door swings open and she's pinned by rich brown eyes – eyes that, until now, she's only seen in pictures. The sleek computer screen didn't do them justice. Her breath itches in her throat. She watches his dark gaze smolder and burn with unsuppressed passion as they undress her Ruby Roxx figure without shame. He caresses her luscious curves and makes love to her.

She feels her skin warm all over. Without a doubt it's turning an embarrassing shade of reddish rose. His eyes flare. As if something inside him snaps, he reaches out and, with near savage strength, pulls her into his embrace. She takes the time to inhale the scent of the ocean on him: the salty residue the water left behind, the sand, the sun, the coconut oil.

Warm soft lips crush down on hers. His kiss: powerful, dominating, soul-draining demands reciprocation – which she gives in abundance. Her body molds itself to his. Her head snaps back to deepen the kiss. Her hands fly in his gorgeous hair nails twisting at the scalp. She sinks her teeth in his plump lower lip making him groan. A sound that sends shivers down her spine; one that makes her curvy hips undulate against his hard frame. His kiss becomes even more heated...Wild! His hold on her tightens.

She likes that she makes him lose his precious control. She feels it. The switch happening. Like a magic button inside of him has been pressed. Trust is now being placed in her hands. She takes it with grace; lets the power of it grow inside of her.

Her fingers release his hair and travels down his powerful back. The feel of his muscles constricting under her touch thrills her. She reaches in front and grabs both side of his shirt collar. She tugs on them ripping the shirt open and sending the tiny discs of buttons flying everywhere. Her hands are finally on him; on his flesh! Her nails start grooving new patterns in his skin, fingers pinch his nipples raw. His chest inflates and deflates rapidly. His breathing is that ragged.

Their kiss is never interrupted. They keep tugging away at the rest of the clothing – his, hers – his cock is swollen and her pussy is dripping wet. The atmosphere is charged. She pushes him onto the glass table in the foyer his butt clunks on the rim of it. Her arms cages in his upper body as her palms land on the wall for support. She rises on her tiptoes and tilts her hips upwards to align her juice-slick entrance to the head of his cock. With her eyes firmly locked on his she connects their bodies as one and slides down his thick erection. The flame burning in his chocolate brown eyes is her reward as she squeezes him in her silken embrace.

She rides him hard and slow. With relish her teeth sink into the flesh of his neck and shoulders at various intervals. The mix of salt and coconut oil and musk and man explodes on her taste buds. The concoction travels in her blood stream, electrifies her skin, and speeds up her tempo. She rides him faster, harder, squeezing his pulsing cock tighter in her wet heat with each climbing bob of her body. Her teeth sinking deeper into any exposed skin they find. She is carefully threading between that precious balance of inflicting pleasure and pain.

From the rumble of his chest to the clenching of his jaw to the way his fingers dig in her flesh and how his cock rocks, twitches and expands against her inner walls she knows pleasure is winning out. She feels it in her core... his need to come. He awaits her command. Only her sweet words will release the torrent.

Her tongue runs the length of his neck. Again her taste buds are assaulted by the powerful aphrodisiac that is *him*. She lingers on his skin drinking more of it in. Twirling and swirling her tongue on his erratically pulsing vein. She starts nibbling his earlobe and then whispers "I'll get down on my knees now and take you in my mouth... and you'll come for me." His entire body shudders in anticipation.

Without preamble she drops to her knees, mouth open in an O, eyes locked on him she takes him to the hilt in one swallow.

Her words resound in his head forming a cage around him. She doesn't need to pin him with her eyes to keep him in place. The fact that she does sends him wild. His muscle strain against the challenge she sets for him. He doesn't break eye contact as he feels the white fire spreading through him. Unable to control the delicious heat that her velvety throat offers; he surrenders. His cock jerks and empties itself inside the greedy wet confines. He stands stock still, honoring her challenge, as her throat muscles keep working: sucking, drinking, and milking him dry. He sees the familiar glint of exhilaration shining in her eyes as the last of his release hits the back of her throat. There is no way to hide how his entire body relaxes under her touch as she releases him and her hands trails up his body. In this moment, she held every inch of him in her magnetic pull and she knew it. All he can do is own up to it. She deserves it.

"What you do to me woman!" He exclaims in a husky voice.

Words she had seen so many times before during their hour long chats and emails. Hearing them spoken for the first time has a simple way of melting her insides. Heat infuses her through and through. Her vision blurs and all she hears is the blood influx as it rushes to keep up with the maddening beating of her heart. Her fingers pinch his nipples hard and scratch his chest. Without giving him time to recover, she crushes her mouth to his knowing full well he would get intoxicated by the taste of his own seed mixed with her essence. As predicated his arms wrap around her in a vice grip. His hands are in her hair; pulling the long black cherry strands. Snapping her neck backwards; deepening the soul-wrecking kiss.

That magic button inside of him has been pressed again. His dominant nature takes over. Her body is swiveled around; torso forced down on the glass table, pebbled nipples pressed against the cool surface become even harder. His fingers find her core and enter swiftly. Three of them fly in and out of her wet swollen folds. Her hair is pulled back even more – arching her neck higher. His cock his pressed to her ass cheeks. His mouth is at the junction of her neck and shoulders. Shivers run down her spine in anticipation.

He doesn't disappoint. His teeth sink down in her tender flesh. His fingers keep rocketing in and out of her sopping pussy lips. "I am going to fuck your ass – hard and deep and slow – so you will remember me there." Her heart pounds, while her blood boils and her pussy tightens. Limbs quake as his rasping voice wraps over her, melts into her. His body presses against her frame as his mouth keeps biting her shoulders and back – moving lower and lower down her spine.

His teeth nibble her upper butt cheek. Saliva drips down her ass crack. The head of his cock rubs it up and down the hot slit. More spit hits her opening. More cock is pushed in between the cheeks. Spit. Push. Spit. Push. Until finally he is seated deeply inside her anal passage. The tight fit of his cock in her barely used entrance is insanely erotic. Especially with the continuous pumping motion of his fingers in her drenched pussy. The push and pull contrast from one hole to the next makes everything inside of her flare up. She feels like quicksilver as taken over her insides.

She feels like a wild wanton panting mess: breathing heavy, abdomen constricting, pussy squeezing the plunging fingers, and ass tightening around the battering cock. Yet there's no helping it. Her body is completely strung out for this man. She knows he feels it... her need to come. She bites on her lower lip to stop the tears from coming. She will hold out for his command. Her body trembles in near pain from the need of it. Her teeth sink deeper in the soft flesh of her lip; so deep the salty metallic taste of blood invades her taste buds. Tears prickle behind her eyes. She blinks them back. There is no way she will cry!

Just when she thinks she will break that vow his honeyed words drip over her "Come for me." He doesn't have time to finish saying them the storm is unleashed. The orgasm rockets through her. Her body bows and jerks with the aftershock of it. She feels his cock push against the tight walls of her ass. He elevates his body over hers sending his engorged cockhead on her G-spot. He rotates on the spongy spot – massaging it counterclockwise; causing a new wave of pleasure to crest inside of her. His thumb pinches her hard swollen clit. Her pussy squirts hot cream in his palm. A feat she knows he doesn't take for granted.

As her pussy is squirting and squirting. He fucks her ass hard and deep. Pulling out completely and plunging back in; the rhythm growing frantic with each thrust. The hand in her hair wraps around the long strands, pulling her head back some more. His teeth connect with the exposed column of her throat. His cock explodes inside her ass.

"What you do to me woman!" He repeats before releasing her.

1-800-XXX

"Hi, my name is Candy, what's your name?"

"Huh, Steve," the nervous voice answered.

"Hmmm, Steve, I like the way your name rolls off my tongue."

There's a shy cough on the other side of line.

Candy waited a few seconds to see if the first time caller, she could always spot the newbie's, would speak up. The silence continued and grew heavy. Her regular practice with a caller is to let them control their experience with her. However, in this case of tortured silence she decided to take charge. She kept things simple and went with phone sex one-oh-one.

"Tell me Steve, what are you wearing."

"A hard-on," he replied in one breath.

"My favorite attire, Steve, *you bad boy*, you do know how to tease a girl."

The breathing across the wire thickened in response to her flirt.

"Is your cock really hard, Steve?" she purred.

"Huh, yeah," he quaked.

"Is it really engorged, like to the point that the veins running the length of it are bulging?" She asked in a breathless voice.

"Oh, y-yeah," he replied between gulping breaths.

"I love your cock Steve. It makes me wet thinking of sliding my hands over it and feeling the full veins pulsing against my palms. I want to touch you *so bad*," she moaned.

When he didn't offer any reply and the panting grew heavier she continued, "Can you touch yourself for me, Steve?"

"S-s-sure," he replied unsteadily.

"I want you to spit in your hands, Steve."

She heard his saliva smack against his palms.

"That's such a turn-on Steve; now slide your slick hands on your erection from root to tip," she pleaded.

The sound of skin on skin reached her ears. Steve's breathing became erratic.

"Tell me Steve; are there beads of pre-come dripping from your cock slit?"

"Yeah," he grunted.

"I bet it's salty and tangy, just as I like it. I want you to taste your come, Steve. Swipe the beads with your pinky finger and suck them in your mouth and tell me if I win the bet," she begged.

The suckling sounds had her nipples hardening. That surprised the hell out of Candy. Wet noises across the wire never affected her this way. Neither did newbies, or any other callers, for that matter. With her voice filled with raw lust, she pleaded "Steve, please tell me how you taste."

"Ca-Candy." He used her phone name for the first time and it actually sent shivers down her spine. "My come is like Crème Anglaise rolling on my tongue and it leaves a briny aftertaste in my throat."

"Hmmm, delicious, just as I knew it would be. Tell me Steve, what would you like to do with this cock of yours?" She asked, hoping to get a glimpse into his inner most fantasy so she could bring him there with her words.

The rhythmic sound subsided and he took several long breathes before answering, "hum." He cleared his throat and tried again, "huh, well, what I'd really want to do is..." He stopped. Candy sensed his shyness and knew like most first time callers he would need to be coaxed into revealing his desires.

"Steve, I am so hot for your cock, *please*, I am begging you, tell me what you want?"

"I am afraid," he whispered.

She loved his innocence and wanted him to feel safe in revealing his fantasy to her.

"Steve, you don't have to be afraid with me. Nothing you'll say will scare me away."

"I saw this picture in a magazine..." He paused to calm his shaking voice.

"It's okay, Steve you can tell me," Candy encouraged.

"I glanced at it, once, twice, fuck! I tore it out of the mag. and kept it under my pillow because it got me so hard thinking about fucking my girlfriend like that..." He hesitated for a second or two and then finally admitted, "but when I finally got up the nerve to show her the picture she called me freak and dumped me." The words rushed out of his mouth.

"Oh, Steve, I am sorry to hear that." Candy felt her heart tighten in her chest. She hated sap stories – for this very reason – they always made her feel soft and gooey and motherly. Steve didn't need *Motherly* right now. He needed to spew his spunk all over his damn hands and she had to bring him there with her words. "Steve, I won't call you a freak. I won't run away. That picture must be pretty awesome. Won't you please describe it to me?" She begged in a throaty voice.

Candy only hoped that her reassuring words would help Steve let go of his reluctance to share, what seemed to be, a powerful fantasy.

"The woman is on her hands and knees, you know doggie style?" He said it as a question and waited for her to reply.

"My favorite style," she purred.

"She has a spiked leather collar around her neck and it's attached to a long linked metal chain..."

Candy immediately understood where the reluctance came from. Steve's dominant side wanted a turn at the wheel, but his reserved nature made it hard for him to describe the submissive female to her. She wanted him to know that the image he painted turned her on – *really turned her on* – her nipples were aching to be touched and her pussy lips were swollen with need.

"Oh, Steve, that sounds so hot. Tell me more about the chain." She sighed.

"The chain. Yeah, okay. It's long. The weave is intricate as if it's been hand knitted. Yet I can tell it's strong and it's attached to a second collar – this one is around the man standing behind the woman."

She whimpered softly. Steve didn't need further encouragement to keep going.

"The man is also wearing wrist cuffs. On each cuff there's a knitted chain. These chains have clamps at the end."

Candy's vaginal muscles clenched a phantom cock. Her nipples tightened and beaded. They wanted to feel those clamps close over them. She used her fingers instead.

"Steve, I am touching myself. My skin is on fire. I want those clamps on me so bad. Tell me, were the clamps tightly in place on her nips in the picture."

"Yes," he replied softly.

Candy's instincts told her that something else about that picture drove him over the edge and to fully give him what he needed to 'get off' she needed to know that *special* something.

"What else in the picture turned you on Steve? Is it her wet and exposed pussy?"

"Huh, no, yes. I don't know," he said in a confused tone.

"It's okay Steve tell me what got your juices flowing."

"The man has his cock buried deep inside her ass and he has a dildo pumping in her pussy."

Candy's body temperature rose. Her skin felt electric. Every touch sent shots of pure lust to her pussy. She pinched her nipples really hard. It didn't provide the relief she wanted. One of her hands trailed down her torso dipped into her jeans and dabbed at her clit. She let out a loud moan.

"Steve, I am so wet. Please, please make me your slave and fuck my ass."

Stunned, he didn't respond. Only his breathing told Candy how much her words turned him on. She continued her submissive role.

"Master, I am yours to take anytime you want."

"Put on your collar. Show me you're my slave," he commanded.

Thrilled that Steve finally let his inner master shine through, Candy knew she could give him control of the call. With pleasure she complied with his request.

"I kneel on the floor. I take the heavy collar and bring it to my throat. I wrap it all around and buckle it as tight as I can."

"Now put on your chain."

"The chain is cold against my palms and hot at the same time. I ease the clip open and slide it in the D ring of my collar and snap it shut."

"Tug on it. Hard."

"I pull on the chain in one sharp move. I feel the leather biting into my neck and hold back the gag reflex."

"Good slave. Give me the chain."

"I close my eyes as I place the chain in my upturned palm and wait for you to pick it up."

"I take the chain from you and test the weight of it in my hands. It feels good. I back up uncoiling it to its full length and sit on the edge of the bed. I command you to stand."

"I lock my eyes on yours as I rise up."

"Take off your pants, slave."

"I unbutton my jeans and grab the zipper tab and begin to unzip..."

"No, turn around, I want to see those sweet cheeks of yours."

"I pivot slowly showing off all my curves until my ass is facing you."

"Good, now take down your pants."

"I roll down the jeans over my hips and bend over to reveal the hot red lacy string riding up my butt cheeks."

"Stop, I want you to push aside the string and show me your openings."

"Yes, Master. I reach from underneath me, gliding my fingers the length of my slit and slip my fingers under the moist material. I slowly tug on the string, releasing it from my butt crack and move it towards my hip."

"Perfect. Now remove the pants."

"I wiggle my bottom until my jeans drop to my knees. I bend over even further to slide them out of my legs one at a time."

"Back up. Bring that sweet ass to me."

"I take a few steps backwards until I hit your knees."

"I grab your ass cheeks. I pinch and squeeze until I see my fingerprints in your soft flesh. I stand up and press my erection against your butt crack. I stay pressed against you as I turn your hips and torso towards the bed and walk behind you. When I have you in the position I want, I command you to burry your face in the mattress."

"Master, I am so hot. Please don't make me wait any longer. Thrust that sweet blade of yours deep inside my ass."

"I smack your bottom, hard. I did not give you permission to speak. Face in the mattress I said."

"I press my cheek deep into the mattress and wait for your next instructions."

"Shit, Candy I am almost there. I want to ram my cock in your ass so bad, but you're not ready yet." Steve's voice quivered with raw need has he stepped out of his character and the picture they were painting with their words.

With a dripping pussy, Candy couldn't stop the orgasm batting against her like waves on rocks and she needed to bring Steve back into his fantasy.

"Master, please I am ready. Dip your cock in my pussy. Use my juices as lube and ease it into my ass. Please. I need you."

Steve regained his composure and acted like a true master.

"You feel my hand slap against your butt cheeks, again and again hitting you in various spots until your bottom is burning under my palm." Steve took in a sharp breath and raised his voice "You're my slave. You speak when I tell you to. Is that clear?"

"Yes, Master," Candy replied in a subdued tone.

"You hear the sound of leather closing around my wrists as well as metal of the buckle as it clicks into place. My hands trail under your torso and firmly grab your breasts. Your nipples are begging for this. I want to hear you moan in pleasure as I clamp your nipples."

"Oh, God, that feels so good." Candy pinched the tip of her nipples harder – imagining them as clamps. The intense sensation rocked her out of balance. She came hard and fast – squirting against the triangle of her g-string. "Oh, yes, yes, I am coming all over myself," she shouted.

"Bad slave! I take the chain and hit it hard across your ass. The movement of my arms yanks on the clamps and they bite deep into your nipples. The pain is instant. Although, I can tell by the way your thighs shake that pleasure quickly follows. Red welts appear on your tender behind. I trace them with my thumb. The movement tugs the chains and clamps. The sweet pressure on your nipples becomes unbearable. You thrust your pelvis outwards slamming your ass against my erection. I slap it again."

Steve paused to take several long deep breaths before speaking again "Such a bad slave, I did not tell you to come. Wipe up your mess and bring your fingers to my mouth," he instructed.

"I reach in my underwear and scoop-up my juices. With my fingers dripping to the knuckles I remove my hand. I twist my wrist backwards and wait for your mouth to close over my sticky fingers."

"My mouth doesn't close over them, it bites down and suck on them – hard. I am teaching you a lesson slave. You come for me. Only me. Only when I tell you to. Got it?"

Too caught-up in the sensations crashing over her body to respond Candy only emitted throaty moans of desire that propelled Steve onwards.

"I tug on your collar chain until I hear you gasp. Who do you come for?"

"You. Only you master," Candy replied in a breathless voice.

"That's right. Say it again."

"I come only for you, Master."

Candy's acquiescing tone drove Steve wild. He needed to come.

"You've been such a bad little slave. I push you down farther into the mattress and thrust my hard cock inside your pussy. I tickle your G-spot with my engorged head."

"Oh, please master, give me more," Candy begs.

"No. I pull out my drenched cock and press it against your butt hole. I spit on your opening and tease it with my thumb. My free hand reaches for the silk pouch lying next to you. I open it and remove a blue silicone penis from its confines."

Candy's breath caught in her throat. Her heart slammed against her rib cage. Sweat ran down her limbs. Her body burned with need.

"Tell me you want this, slave."

"Oh God, yes, I want it. I want it deep inside of my pussy as much as I want your cock in my ass."

"I ease my cock between your ass cheeks. My engorged head disappears in your hot opening. I thrust the dildo in your pussy. You scream in ecstasy as I push my cock farther inside your ass."

"Oh, Master, that feels so fucking good. Please don't stop," Candy panted.

"I glide the silicone penis in out of your pussy in time with each thrust of my cock in your ass. I feel the dildo sliding against the thin membranes separating your two openings. The sweet pressure of your muscles tightening around my cock makes it swell inside of your ass. My balls are hard and pressing tight one against the other. They slam against your butt as I drive my cock farther inside that sweet ass of yours."

"Master, please tell me to come. I want to come so bad."

"Not yet. Again and again I slam my rock hard balls against your butt. The dildo is thrusting in and out of your swollen pussy lips. Your thighs shake against mine as I keep rocking my cock in the deep hot confines of your ass. I increase the tempo of both my cock and dildo. Faster and faster, I thrust into your openings. I feel the blood rushing down to my cock. It's pulsating inside of you."

"Oh, yeah, yeah, please don't stop," Candy rubbed her clit to the same tempo Steve described. Her lower abdomen constricted in quick succeeding motion. The orgasm painfully hovered over her... She had to wait for him to give her permission.

He didn't make her wait long.

"I pull my cock out of your ass at the same time as I slide the silicone penis out of your pussy lips. I ram three fingers inside of you. I press them against your g-spot and drive my cock in your ass. My cock is full and ready to burst. Come slave. Come now."

They panted and grunted in unison.

In her six years as a phone sex operator she'd never gotten so caught up in the role play before. She scanned her body with her unbelieving eyes. She felt depleted and electrified at the same time.

"Oh. My. God. Steve, my tank top is rolled down to my navel, my jeans are hanging loosely around my hips, my soaked panties are pushed aside, exposing my dripping pussy to the air conditioning vent just above my chair."

"Candy, I am still gushing. I never knew it could be this exhilarating to take charge like that."

"My body is still vibrating from the sexual aftershock. You were a good Master, Steve. Don't ever be afraid of that."

"I'll call you whenever I need a willing slave," he said with smile in his voice.

"Good night, Steve."

"Good night, Candy."

Candy removed her head set and placed it in her top drawer. She straightened out her clothes and dug under her desk for her tote bag; she slung it over her shoulder and shut-off her station.

***

When Amber, aka Candy, walked into her bedroom later that night she found her lover asleep on his back. His arms were thrown over his head, his penis stood proud; fully erect.

She quickly removed her clothes and tossed them in the hamper. Without a sound she straddled him and plunged down on his erection. His eyes flew open. His pelvis thrust upwards.

"No," she told him as she move up and released his cock.

"No fair," he said as he tried to pull her back down.

She grabbed his hands, held them in place against her hips as she turned on her knees.

"Are you sure?" Her lover asked in an awed tone. He knew she only liked doggy style if he rode her ass, and, she so rarely offered him this privilege.

"Yes, Steve. Tonight, I need you to fuck my ass. Fuck it now!"

The Nyotaimori Model

In one clean thrust Reginald's quivering member sank into Miss Evelyn's sex. She cried out in pain as the thick blade pierced her membrane. Reginald stilled. "It's okay, my sweet. We'll take it nice and slow," he cooed as his fingers plied at her soft breasts. His mouth covered hers offering sultry kisses. When her breathing grew rapid he started moving within her. As soon as he saw her eyes gloss over with pleasure he picked up the tempo.

"Amanda."

He pulled out of her warmth and plunged back in again. Her pelvis moved with him; meeting his every thrust. Reginald could see that Miss Evelyn finally surrendered to the delicious waves of pleasure crashing over. He loved that she behaved in such a wanton way.

"Amanda."

He pushed farther into her. She cried out in ecstasy. Again and again he slid his manhood in and out of her silken channel. She became a quivering panting mess beneath him. Watching her eyes dilate and fill with raw passion made the fire in his loins explode.

"A-A-A-mmmannda!"

Amanda tore herself away from her book and turned to face her roommate. "What," she said with more force than necessary.

"Phone," Becky replied in a petulant tone.

"Bugger," she uncurled herself from her comfy reading chaise and headed to the kitchen. Amanda snatched-up the receiver from the counter top "Hello," she said unable to hide her irritation.

"Miss Galloway?"

"Yes."

"This is Mr. Mojito from Nyotaimori Express."

"Good evening, Mr. Mojito, how can I help you?" Her tone cooled. From zero to sixty it changed to her professional one with just the right hint of sweetness mixed in it because her clients liked it that way.

"We have a booking tomorrow night at the Escalade. The client made it crystal clear that he wants you to be his model."

"Who is the client?" Amanda asked even though she already knew that only one name from her rolodex had enough money to book the Escalade and pay the heavy premium to select his model – the horse whispering billionaire.

"Mr. O'Malley." He paused to emphasize the importance of this revelation. "From my understanding, he's reserved the entire upper floor of the Escalade for tomorrow evening. Will you accept the booking?"

Amanda's heart raced a little when Mr. Mojito confirmed her suspicion. Nothing could make her pass up this booking – it promised to be a *very* special one indeed. Her cheeks flamed at the thoughts that invaded her mind, thoughts that could lose her, her job if her employer ever found out. She felt proud of herself when she managed to keep her voice cool and calm when she replied.

"Yes sir, at what time is the prep crew going to arrive?"

"19h00; dinner will begin at 20h00."

"I'll see you there sir. Good night."

"Good night Miss Galloway."

Amanda placed the receiver back in its cradle. She felt her heart race in her chest. WOW! Nearly a year abroad this time and her Irish stud – 6'2" of hard sun-tanned muscles, soft hands, honeyed voice, and piercing blue eyes – now back in town. Oh, this promised to be so much better than her smutty novel.

***

"Ah, Miss Galloway, how lovely to see you again," Mr. Mojito greeted her as she entered.

"Mr. Mojito. It's always a pleasure to see you sir," she replied.

"Tonight's menu will include a variety of our traditional maki rolls and sashimis, tuna tataki and konoha. The dessert course will be our famous amai ai. Miss Galloway, we're ready any time you are."

"Thank you, Mr. Mojito I'll just be a minute."

Amanda entered the posh sitting room and discarded her clothes. She looked at her figure in the full length mirror. Her breasts reminded her of oversized peaches. Amanda admired the cream complexion of her skin and how it made the peachiness of her areolas all the more mouth watering. As her eyes travelled down her body, she felt proud of herself. She kept her stomach flat and toned and her long legs shapely and athletic with her daily yoga and jogging routine.

As a Nyotaimori model or as Becky likes to call her – the naked sushi table – her profession made it mandatory for her to keep her body in tip-top shape and hair free at all times. At the beginning of week she'd spent the day at the salon getting the regular work done: waxing, facial, manicure, pedicure and so on. As a result, her skin looked as soft as silk – flawless.

Ready for this, she stepped out of the room and climbed on the linen clad oak table that Mr. Mojito set a few inches away from the circling bay window overlooking the Ottawa River. The city skylights in the far off background offered a breathtaking sunset view with a mix of ocher and indigo. For a minute she felt like if she'd stepped into another world.

"Miss Galloway, please lie down and we'll get started."

The sound of Mr. Mojito's voice brought her back to the present. Amanda did as requested and shimmied once or twice until she found her happy place on the table. Mr. Mojito and his assistant spent nearly an hour decorating her body with all the menu items. The only additions were the three heather spikes that Mr. O'Malley sent earlier that evening. These were delicately placed across her nipples and clitoris. Once they declared her a piece of art they lit the long white tapers and exited the room. Amanda closed her eyes and counted her breaths. She'd reached sixty seven breaths when the atmosphere in the room changed.

The sensual tension grew heavier.

He's arrived.

"You're even lovelier than I remembered," he murmured in his lilting accent as his fingers traced the contours of her body.

His soft touch sent shivers down her spine.

He settled himself in the chair at her feet. He bent his head and ran his tongue from the tip of her toe to the top of her foot where sat a spicy tuna roll. He opened his mouth wide and scraped her skin with his teeth as he nibbled on the roll. His hot breath on her skin felt exquisite. Her nipples hardened. Moisture grew between her legs. Done with the roll his tongue moved upwards to suck in the piece of raw salmon that covered her talus. The sweet pressure of his suction ignited sparks of electricity in her veins.

"Mmmmm, delicious," he purred.

Amanda didn't even question what he found delicious. She knew that he referred to her – her skin, her taste.

His lips and tongue continued their upwards path – licking, kissing, nibbling and sucking. They moved slowly up the length of her right calf. After he devoured the California roll sitting on top her knee, he kissed her limb and started the same sweet torturing process with her left foot, calf and knee. By the time his mouth finished nibbling the piece of tuna tataki on her left knee; Amanda's nerve endings were as raw as the pieces of sushi decorating her body. Her insides trembled with a deep-rooted need of him. Her slit glistened. Her nipples hardened and tightened to the point that it bordered on the threshold of pleasure and pain. She could barely keep her breathing in check.

"Such beautiful skin. Soft. Cool," he said in his special hushed tone as his fingers drew little circles on her knee.

The fire deep in her belly rose to a scorching heat. She knew that she could get burned by this man. Yet, she didn't care. She wanted him. Agony gnawed her raw because his fingers just lay there, unmoving, almost as in still repose on her knee. She held her breath to see what he would do next. Her heart nearly jumped out of her chest when his fingers glided down her inner thigh. Slowly, they floated over her labia and rested on the stem of the heather spike.

Her clit throbbed in anticipation.

He twirled the heather spike. The tiny leaves flicked against her hardened clit again and again as the spinning spike turned between his thumb and forefinger. Overwhelmed by the incredible sensation she concentrated on just feeling. She felt everything – her pulsing clit, her dripping core, her tightening belly, her vaginal muscles contracting hard and fast. Unable to hold herself in check anymore she came in long heavy squirts

"Aye, that's my lass," he said as he plunged his fingers inside her clenching pussy. "Give me more love," he purred with his fingers slamming into her, reaching deeper with every thrust.

She flexed her neck backwards. Arched her back to the point that some of the sushi flew off her torso and screamed in ecstasy as her juices abundantly flowed over his knuckles.

"Mmmmm, delicious," he exclaimed with a ring of satisfaction in his voice as he pulled out his fingers and brought them to his mouth. He sucked each finger clean.

Amanda fell back down on the table. A sentence from her smutty novel popped into her mind "*She became a quivering panting mess...*" Her lips turned up in a smile as big as a Cheshire cat when she realized just how accurate that sentence described her current state. The sound of his footsteps made her pulse skyrocket. He reached the head of the table and stood there, with a tent in his pants, mere inches away from her salivating mouth.

"You want this, don't you love." He made it a statement not a question.

He moved closer to her, stroking his impressive length over the wool material of his pants – up, down, squeezing the base and up again. Finally, he grabbed the zipper tab and drew it down. His fitted designer briefs hugged his erection to perfection. His thumb slid underneath the elastic and pulled the briefs downwards.

His cock sprung free.

Her lips parted.

He plunged into her mouth in one swift move of his pelvis. She took him in all the way to the back of her throat. He slipped his cock out and thrust it back in. In and out, his cock plunged.

"I love fucking your mouth," he grunted as his fingers dug into her hair holding her head in place.

He plunged hard and deep – so deep that his balls were smacking against her chin. Amanda took short breathes through her nose and relished in the feel of the long, thick cock caressing her tongue. She sucked hard pressing it against the roof of her mouth. The bulging veins running the length of him pulsed against her teeth. She reduced the sucking pressure and twirled her tongue round and round his thick shaft. With a twist of his pelvis his cock pushed deeper in her throat. She held back the gag reflex and opened to accommodate his girth. He pumped once, twice more and gushed salty tangy liquid down her throat. Greedily, she swallowed every ounce of it.

He pulled out and lowered his lips to hers. His tongue invaded her mouth and dueled with hers. The sushi forgotten he pulled her up into his arms, crushed her body with his. He grabbed her waist and moved her further up on the table. He climbed on the spot she'd just deserted. He pushed his head between her legs and inhaled. The smell of her sex – rich, musky, sweet – intoxicated his senses. He kissed her inner thigh. His mouth left a trail of kisses on her skin as his tongue glided closer and closer to her glistening slit. His nostrils flared. He couldn't wait any longer he licked, up and down her pussy lips.

So sweet; the taste of her left him impatient and hungry for more. His tongue parted her wet lips and plunged deep inside her core. He drank and drank her sweet nectar. Her pelvis undulated, pushed up and out, bringing his tongue fully inside. Flicking it this way and that he left no corner untouched, unsavored. Inch by inch he pulled his tongue out of her molten core and teased her hardened clit. He licked, sucked, nipped until her pelvis thrashed against his face.

"Aye, that's my sweet lass," he purred against it.

Her hot cream poured onto his tongue. Like a starved tomcat he lapped it all up. He lifted his head from between her legs and pulled himself up until his knees rested there. He drew her onto his lap.

"Ride your stallion love," he whispered in her ear.

She sank down on his erection. She closed her eyes enjoying the feel of him deep inside of her – stretching her to the limit.

"Ride lass, ride," he pleaded.

In slow motion she moved up and down his blade.

"Ahhh, you're killin' me."

She picked up the tempo, rising up until only his cockhead remained within her embrace, and, then drove herself down to sheath him to the hilt. Time after time she impaled herself on his cock. His hands gripped her hips; his mouth captured one of her bobbing nipples. He twirled his tongue around the lengthened bead sending shocks of pleasure straight to her clit.

"Ahhhhhhhhh," she moaned.

"You feel so good. You're all hot and wet. So wet," he groaned.

He tilted his pelvis upwards meeting her downwards pushes. The head of his cock hit her G-spot. He pushed farther in pressing hard against her sweet spot. She moaned deep in her throat as the dam broke. Hot juices flowed over the tight skin of his cock. She slammed her butt cheeks on his thighs and squeezed his cock between her swollen lips sending him over the edge. His spunk gushed out and mixed with hers.

"I've missed you Mrs. O'Malley," he whispered.

"I've missed you to Mr. O'Malley," she breathed back and added, "remember my stallion... no one knows I am not Miss Galloway."

"Aye, I remember, but I don't have to like it!" He growled. "I would scream it at the top of my lungs at the Irish Derby that you are mine... If you'd let me that is." The bitter undercurrent of this tone told her just how deeply the last two years have hurt him. Shame filled her core.

"Connor, I want that to. More than anything, but ..."

"...Come with me," he pleaded in his persuasive Irish lilt.

"Can I really? Are you ready to answer all the questions?"

"Aye, I'll face them and anything else. I don't care a whit that you're nearly twelve years my senior. I've told you that from the start. You're the one who seems to be preoccupied by the age difference. You think my parents will find it scandalous? Love, my mum and dad would be elated to know that I'm happily married and very, very much in love with my wife. I want to introduce to my family and show you my world. Let me! Quit your job. Come with me. Be my wife. Not just for one night. Forever. Aye, I am asking for always"

His eyes, like blue fire searched her face with such intensity she felt like their depths reached her soul. Sure that he could read her thoughts, she let them wander.

When she'd met him two years ago while touring Ireland she'd fallen head over heels for him. Never in her wildest dream had she imagined that he would want her. Well ok, *maybe in her wildest*, but she never expected them to come true. Nearly thirty-six at the time and he'd just turned twenty-three, living life to the fullest, he traveled from one corner of the world to the next bestowing his gentle gift with horses as needed.

He'd pursued her with adamant fervor, wilting away her resolve with his bold show of his desire for her. It started at a filled to brim pub in Dublin where he upstaged the band and took centre stage. His pursuit continued when he followed her across the land and serenaded her on a crowded Galway beach. It didn't stop there, in front of hundreds of tourists he cried out his love for her at the Blarney Castle and then kissed the blue stone so he may gain the greatest eloquence to win his lady's heart.

She'd thought him mad – but her heart – oh, her heart found him to be the essence of perfection. How could it not? With his never ending blue eyes, sleek glossy black hair, broad shoulders, hard sinuous muscles that formed his torso and dipped down his trim waist and continued on to shape the beautiful curves of his bulging thighs and calves. After such a flourish and with her heart racing a hundred miles a minute, it's no wonder that, when his lips claimed hers in a kiss she abandoned her qualms and fell into him. She fell so hard that he married her in a small church in Mayo County before she returned to Canada.

Coming back home *alone* nearly killed her. Spending the next two years with only seeing glimpses of him, her beloved husband tortured her. Finally, here and now, she felt ready to give up her silly reservations. Who cared if she approached forty, and, he only neared thirty – five years south of it to be exact! Those silly details didn't matter to her anymore.

She loved him.

He adored her.

Why had she let such a foolish notion such as age get in the way of their happiness? The resolve of her decision shone in her eyes. She knew that no words were needed. He could read her message loud and clear – I am yours, forever.

With a radiant smile on her face she nuzzled against her husband's neck deeply breathing in the exotic scent of him. The rich smell of well oiled leather with undertones of sagebrush and hay and peppermint all the horsey smells she had come to recognize and long for. Mixed in with the earthy smell of *him* on top of the pungent aroma of their sex created such a heady combination – One of home.

Amanda couldn't be happier.

The Forbidden Fruit

The moment Charlotte showed up at the door of his shoebox apartment, with brimmed red eyes, he should have known that his heart would be in jeopardy.

She'd thrown herself into his arms and begged him, "Please Damian; let me stay the night with you."

"You can go freshen up while I get the cot out of closet."

"Damian," her voice had trembled when she said his name. "I know I am asking a lot of you, but could you, just this once, sleep with me in your bed." Her face had been flaming red when those words had spilled out of her mouth.

Dumbfounded by her request he had been frozen in thought. *Is she asking me to be her lover for the night?* His heart had somersaulted in his chest and then plummeted.

"I am not ready to be alone. I know you wouldn't try anything. I feel safe with you."

He had wanted to scream that he would try everything to keep her in his bed and life forever. Instead he'd reassured her. "Ah, Charlotte, of course I wouldn't try anything. I promise I'll keep you safe."

She'd flashed him a grateful smile and strolled to his bathroom across the hall. He'd hopped into bed, glued himself to the wall and pretended to be asleep when she'd padded back into his room.

What I am supposed to do? I gave Charlotte my word to keep her safe... even if in end it means that I have to protect her from my own set of carnal desires.

Damian Stone quietly talked to himself while he pitted his will against his most natural needs. From the root of his hair, to his fisted knuckles and balled up toes, his rigid muscles were drenched with the sweat of his effort. All his concentration focused on keeping his body in this stiff pose as he breathed through clenched teeth.

I know she doesn't realize what this is doing to me. Shit, I wish she could fathom how much will power I am exhorting here. Arrrgggg! It's driving me insane – with her curled up like that next to me on my tiny bed. Her perfect curves looking invitingly soft and warm... all I'd have to do is move an inch and I'd be able to touch and savor her sweet alabaster skin. He balled his fingers tighter into his palms. It did not stop his circling thoughts.

What kind a cluster fuck did I get myself into? Honestly! It's as if my brains left me the moment she walked into my life. I want her – heart, body and soul. But she's never been or ever will be mine to take. He reminded himself for the hundredth time.

Breathing in her rose petal scent inflamed all of his senses making it that much more difficult for him to keep a lid on his primal temptations. *This is my personal hell* he thought grimly, as she shifted closer to him pressing her sexy ass to his thigh. The reaction – immediate – his shaft went rock hard. She kept wiggling in her sleep, as if something in her dreams prevented her from resting peacefully. She breathed in short gasps. Sobs escaped her lips. *Should I wake her?* He wondered as he glanced over his shoulder.

Damian's heart raced in his chest when he saw the quilt had slipped down her body exposing the sexy low cut black lace camisole she wore. He couldn't peel his eyes off the rising and falling of the milky white breasts underneath the sheer garment. Her peachy nipples were hard and extended. He wanted to suck them in the heat of his mouth. His tongue scraped against his teeth, eager to come out and trace the outline of the succulent forbidden fruit next to him.

He bit down hard on his straying tongue and tasted his own blood. *Ouch!* Not a good idea he mused while cursing himself silently. He started to understand that doing the right thing didn't always equal easy. There were most definitely consequences to his earlier decisions. Decisions that were now putting his own sanity in question!

He'd been pasted to wall for the past two hours with her delicate form pressed against him. In this situation, even a saint would have a raging hard-on. He ground his teeth in frustration! He felt doomed to endure the constant sexual current flowing through him, begging to be released. It didn't help that Charlotte kept tossing and turning. Each time she moved, the quilt moved with her, exposing more and more of her enticing flesh. His pulse skyrocketed when he noticed the string of black lace riding up her butt cheeks. His cock pulsed in anticipation.

Oh shit, I want to push aside that tiny string with my tongue and nibble those lovely cheeks. Lick her puckered opening until its wet and slick and then bury my hot cock deep inside that sexy ass of hers. Run my hand between her thighs. Flick my fingers over her clit. Thrust in and out of her anus until she screams in ecstasy and her juices squirt out into my hand as the orgasm crashes through her. His erection throbbed painfully.

Having her near at hand, and, almost naked at that made the sexual charge too much to bear. He extended his fingers one by one. Damian reached out. His index finger stopped a mere millimeters above her G-string. *I can't do this. Charlotte came to me for support and understanding. Not for primal sex.* His cock jumped in frustration of being denied the hot confines of the perfect cheeks pressing so close to him.

Damian shifted his eyes to his engorged purple head peeking out of his boxers. He let his hand drop to his waist – pulled out his hot cock and let his strong fingers circle the base of his erection. *Fuck! I shouldn't be doing this. She's driving me insane. It's either this or I take her like a wild animal – pumping in and out of her sweet ass in a cruel, gruelling, fast and hard pace. I can't do that to her.*

He closed his eyes and let himself imagine her hands on him as he increased the pressure around his cock and stroked it from root to tip.

His breath quickened.

The image in his mind shifted.

He pictured Charlotte's knees on either side of his head with her delicious derrière pressed against his face; the perfect position to fuck her butt hole with the tip of his tongue and to have his fingers sliding in and out of her wet pussy. To have her sexy lips wrapped around his long, hard cock. To thrust it deep inside her throat, making her feel it pulse there, filling every inch of her mouth.

The rated R image drove Damian wild. His hand moved up and down his rock hard erection with vigor. His balls squeezed tight one against the other. His muscles trembled as a violent orgasm shot through him.

Hot semen spilled out in his palms.

Trickled down his fingers.

Dripped on the bed.

Damian panted from the power still vibrating through him. For tonight, the fantasy of her seemed to assuage the beast within; he fell asleep with a satisfied smile on his face.

Up for Grabs

Sydney Foster couldn't wait for this stupid night to end.

When she agreed to this charade she thought it would be glamorous to be rubbing elbows with the "who's who" of today's high political society. To be among women in elegant evening gowns and tall dark handsome men in tuxedos, to inhale exotic perfumes floating in the air and be mesmerized by sparkling jewels that would make even the royal family envious. She'd been so sure that one of her dreams would finally come true.

More like a nightmare.

A conservative, stuffy, and downright *boring* one at that! While it's true she'd been assigned a spot in the media line; the press, it seems, would be granted fifteen minutes of questioning at the end of the evening – yippee! Her eyes rolled skywards of their own accord at the *thrilling* thought. No wonder Cass wanted her to fill-in for the night.

Cassandra Waters, her childhood best friend had asked her, no, begged her to take her place at this evening's event. She'd even provided Sydney with the WORKS: gorgeous dress and shoes, make-up, perfume, exquisite jewellery and most importantly her press credentials.

Sydney of course had no trouble impersonating Cassandra. Both had the same ivory complexion, long wavy chestnut hair, green slanted eyes, high cheek bones, full mouths and unless they were side by side no one really noticed an inch or two difference in height or even a couple of pounds in weight. Sydney had been completely swept-up off her feet by this proposal that she didn't even stop to question as to why Cassandra wanted to pass up this event. She'd just grabbed the opportunity and ran with it.

At the doors of the Westin's Hotel grandest ballroom, Sydney flashed the press badge with confidence. Promptly a spot opened for her amongst the other reporters waiting for a scandalous event to occur. So far, she witnessed the exchange of polite conversation as the rich and powerful circled around the room from cluster to cluster. Cass had not been specific about what to look for. Her only words were "*don't worry Syd, you'll know it when you see it*" and by "*it*" she meant the something to write about.

Sydney wanted to give up this silly assignment and go home when she spotted him across the room. Martial Gibbs, the newly elected counsel-man – provocative, forward-thinking – he shook things up in Parliament. His pro same sex marriage views had stirred up quite a bit of trouble on the Hill not to mention all the speculations floating around the city regarding *his* personal tastes. Every eligible bachelor and bachelorette in Ottawa hoped to bag him, *so to speak.*

Sydney couldn't stop herself from admiring Counsellor Gibbs's dark hair and broad shoulders nor could she ignore his finely sculpted long legs and slim waist under her eyelashes as she watched him make his way across the room. She let her eyes travel to his upper body. The un-buttoned tuxedo jacket let her glimpse a snug-fitted dress shirt over a perfect set of abs. She felt herself blush and quickly lifted her eyes higher. His ice-blue eyes locked on hers holding her captive.

How did he get over here so fast? She wondered when she realized that only a few inches separated them and that his hand now lay extended towards her in invitation. She lifted her hand and watched, eyes growing as large as saucers, has his hand closed over hers. Sparks of electricity burst through her veins has he pulled her out of the media pack and onto the dance floor. His arms encircled her waist with ease and confidence. Her hands trembled as she felt the quiet power hidden in the sinuous muscles of his arms and shoulders. With her head perfectly settled in the nook of his neck. One deep breath is the only thing it took. The scent of his after shave a clean masculine musk – so intoxicating – she could have drowned in it. Sydney closed her eyes and let herself be led around the dance floor. She felt goose bumps at the nape of her neck when his hands trailed down her spine.

Cassandra had a thing for low-cut, beaded halter tops, opened back dresses. This little crimson number she left Sydney proved that. Earlier that evening when Sydney stepped into the dress she felt awed by how it hugged her curvy figure with perfection. The halter top with its build-in push up bra and low cut V offered more cleavage then she felt comfortable with.

Sydney quivered as his hands continued to move up and down her back. Her nipples hardened against the soft material of her dress. Aching to be touched, she parted her lips and ran her tongue along his neck. His hands lowered below her waist and pulled her buttocks closer to him. Moisture grew between her legs when she felt every inch of his erection. The length and bulk of him made her vulva throb with anticipation.

On impulse she breathed in his ear "Let's get out of here."

**

While dead on his feet, Martial Gibbs, didn't want to attend another long political gala where the main topic of conversation would be his sexual preferences. He knew that not making an appearance at this shin-ding would only fuel the wagging tongues. Resigned, he walked into the venue with a smile plastered on his face. The conservatively decorated and illuminated grand ballroom didn't surprise him. The jazz band played one quiet number after another. After almost two hours of circling around the room making polite conversation and dodging several roaming hands, Martial just wanted to call it a night. His smile brightened when he scanned the line of reporters.

In mid sweep his eyes stopped. Martial's gaze settled on a very attractive young woman in a sizzling red dress. He dropped his sight to the floor; her shoes where the same crimson color as her dress. His eyes traced her legs up and up. The dress flared around her knees in a playful way. Enthralled, his gaze moved upward, the trim-fitted dress embraced the curves of her hips and hugged her waist. His balls tighten uncomfortably when his eyes settled on her chest. The beaded halter-top of the dress sparkled with crystals. Almost like if the garment offered him her voluptuous breasts on a silver platter.

His mouth watered. He lifted his head to set his eyes on her face. Her red painted lips, curved into a polite smile, were so sexy. In an instant the posh ballroom disappeared. *A witch, she must be a witch.* A sudden flash of those lips wrapped around his engorged cock had his temperature rising. His breathing grew heavy. Martial shook his head to remove the X-rated image from his mind. It didn't work. This young woman exuded sensuality and he fell under her spell. Truth be told, he felt enraptured by it. His eyes locked on hers. They were green, like the rolling hills of Scotland and he walked right into them.

There's no way that this incredible woman will want me, he thought as he made his way across the room. His heart pounded in his chest as he extended his hand to her in invitation. The softness of her hand in his and the look of astonishment in her eyes gave him the confidence he needed to pull her onto the dance floor. He drew her close to him and wrapped his arms around her waist. The smell of her perfume, a perfect combination of ripe peaches and white musk, intoxicated his senses. He wanted to taste that mixture on his tongue and savour it forever. When his hand met the bare flesh of her back, sparks of electricity shot through him.

I have to get a hold of myself or else she'll think I am complete pervert and...

Martial's train of thought cut short when her tongue ran along his neck. He'd never met a woman this bold. It really turned him on! No longer able to keep his wild attraction a secret, his hands cupped her derrière and brought her pelvis closer to his ensuring that she felt his growing shaft. Her warm breath on his ear lobe and the sultry timbre of her voice lit a fire in his gut when she suggested "Let's get out of here."

"I have a room," he heard himself whisper.

"What are we waiting for?" She breathed back.

Martial twirled her around in his arms. With her firmly planted in front of him, hiding the growing bulge in his pants, he led them out of the stuffy room.

***

In the lobby, he stopped by the front desk to pick-up his room key. The rectangular plastic tab felt heavy in his palm as they made their way to the elevator doors. The feel of her in his arms, warm and soft, made his pulse skyrocket. He felt like a teenager going out on a date for the first time. Martial didn't know why this young woman had such an effect on him. He just knew that he feared of letting her go.

This is insane! All I have to do is untangle my arm for a second and push a damn button.

Just as he'd talked himself into releasing her, her slim index finger reached out and pushed the Up arrow. His eyes lifted above the doors and watched the floor numbers flash in red. Suddenly, he felt impatient to get the beautiful creature in his arms behind the doors of his Suite before she could change her mind and walk away from him.

Impatience and heat nearly drove him insane. His entire being felt afire it's something that made him feel off kilter. At the same the same time it exhilarated him to be so hot for her, his hands were twitching to untie the knot of her dress and to have her magnificent breasts spill out of it. He balled his fingers into his palms and kept watching the little red numbers decrease. Anticipation filled him. Finally, the doors swished open. They stepped in, his fingers relaxed, and he pushed the top floor button.

Sydney's heart pounded in her chest. The city's most sought after bachelor wanted her. The solid heat pressed against her back assured her of that. She couldn't help but smile impishly. She could see the headline now *Counsellors Gibbs straight after all.* Her body tingled with sexual anticipation. The feel of his cock on the small of her back enticed her in the extreme. It made her wet, thinking about having that fine specimen inside of her – stretching her. She bit her lip in impatience.

Why is it taking so long? I want to rip open his dress shirt and run my hands all over him. I want to make his nipples pucker up; harden into small beads in my mouth.

The doors finally slid opened. They stepped out of the elevator. Martial led them down the corridor to his room. He slid the plastic tab in the card slot and removed it before the light flashed green. His hand trembled when he tried again. This time he waited for the little green light before turning the knob.

Sydney had never walked in the Rideau Suite before; the sleek richness of it all stunned her. The chic and modern furniture, the colors of burnt orange, slate gray and stark white, though an odd combo in her mind, fit well with the dark cheery wood tables and glass lamps. The plush slate gray area rug of the sitting room with bright white wavy lines running the length of it also fit decor. The fully stocked wet bar on which sat a crystal vase overflowing with wild orchids finished the room to perfection. She gulped, hoping to swallow the sudden knot of apprehension that lodged itself in her throat.

Holly Shit! He's so out of my league.

To prove to herself that she still held control, she strolled over to the heavy looking jade drapes and glided them on their pole until the bay window stood completely bare. She felt his eyes devouring her silhouette as she stood there looking at the Ottawa skyline. Slowly, she turned to face him. He reached for the bottle of champagne and the blown glass flutes – that she'd somehow missed.

"Would you like some?"

"I'd love some."

Her voice sounded like wind chimes, every tone of it vibrated through him playing havoc on his already raging hormones. With shaking hands, he popped the cork of the bottle. Bubbles spilled out onto his fingers and dripped to the posh carpeting. He stared at her with a sheepish look on his face and returned his attention to the bubbling wine.

As he started to pour it into the awaiting flutes, Sydney acted on impulse. She took the few steps that were separating them and with a confidence she didn't entirely feel, she took his hand into hers and slowly brought it up to her lips. She slid out her tongue and ran it along the edge of his index finger tasting the crisp cold wine on him.

Martial's pulse skyrocketed once more. He clumsy placed the champagne bottle on the side table. Her tongue reached the tip of his index. With her eyes locked on his; she twirled once then twice before sucking his finger into the hot confines of her mouth. His erection pushed painfully against the zipper of his slacks; begging for same attention.

"Give me those lips," he pleaded.

She released his finger at his request and turned up her face to him. His mouth scooped down and ravaged hers. The moment his lips touched hers, every nerve in his body ignited. He groaned in her mouth. Sydney felt truly empowered to make these bold moves and have him respond in such a way. Relishing in her new found power, she glided her tongue seductively over his. He bent her neck a little and deepened their kiss. His tongue explored every hidden treasure her mouth offered.

Breathless their mouths broke apart. Staring into each other's eyes, they saw the raw passion they had for one another. Each of them felt the intensity of that wanting wrap around them, cocooning them in a ball of fiery need that couldn't be denied. The sex charged bubble left Sydney wanting more. Her breath caught in her throat when he lowered his mouth to hers and traced her lips with his tongue. She let out a soft moan when he slipped it into her mouth.

Sydney panted with need; his mouth hot on hers. She desperately wanted to feel that busy tongue of his on her neck, her breasts, her navel on her throbbing clit. Unable to withstand the rush of desire within her, she ran her hands over the rough wool material of his jacket. She grabbed his lapels and pushed them aside. Her fingers slipped underneath his silk tie. With ease she loosened the knot and worked the tie free of his neck. Her busy fingers moved downwards and started fumbling with the buttons of his dress shirt. Impatient to get her hands on his naked flesh, she cursed the tiny discs because she couldn't work them through the small openings.

This daring woman knew exactly what she wanted and she went for it with a delightful abandon. Heat flooded over him when her fingers awkwardly tried to manipulate the miniscule buttons of his shirt. He didn't trust his own fingers to be able to work through the long downward series. Wanting to feel her fingers curl into his chest, he bunched up a couple of inches of material on each side of his shirt and tore it open. Not enough; he wanted to feel her hands everywhere on him. He shrugged off his jacket and the ruined shirt. Leaving his torso completely bare and at her disposal.

She did not disappoint him. In slow motion her nails ran through the coarse hair of his chest all the way down to his navel. The tip of her nails moved upward and circled his nipples; working them until they became hard as pebbles. She broke off the kiss and let her lips travel down his neck, pressing soft kisses along his Adam's apple, his clavicles, his pectorals and finally her tongue flicked his harden nipples. She licked them each at a time, sucking them against the roof of her velvety mouth. His breathing grew ragged as she abandon his nipples and let her tongue trail down.

Her fingers clasped around his belt buckle. She pulled at it and removed the tab from its hole. He felt let a firecracker ready to explode as she slowly unzipped his pants. They fell to floor; mesmerized in place he didn't step out of them. Her fingers slipped under the elastic of his briefs and touched the purple head of his cock. The warmth of her breath moving down from his navel drove him mad. His penis throbbed against her hand.

"Mmmm so eager for my touch, a girl could get drunk on that," she murmured as her hand slid his briefs down under his ass and captured the tip of his erection into that sexy mouth of hers. She flicked her tongue along the ridge of his purple head.

His fingers dipped into her hair and curled around the heavy locks. "That feels so good," he grunted. She opened her throat and took him in to the hilt. The sweet suction she kept as her head bobbed up and down his erection drove him over the edge. His muscle trembled as he ejaculated in her mouth.

Sydney released his semi erect penis and turned her attention to his balls. She licked each of them thoroughly and gently suckled them. Even if he just came in her mouth, she knew that he would become hard as a rock again. Sydney felt elated. Being bold and daring with a man definitely paid off. To see, *feel*, her partner's undeniable need for her – incredible. His body reacted, in a very sexy way, to her every touch. She gave his balls one last lick and slowly stood to her full height.

With his fingers still tangled in her hair, Martial crushed her against him. He released her hair and let his fingers move down to her neck. He felt her pulse quickened at his touch. His fingers worked the knot of her dress free and he peeled it off her body in slow motion. Her breasts were full and round and perfect. His mouth watered at the sight of her darkened nipples – hard, erect – ready to be sucked.

The way his eyes were drinking in the milkiness of her skin made her feel like a Goddess. She knew she should have been shy about being half naked, not only in front of him, but in front of the bay window. To her surprise, she felt deliciously excited about the possibility of being watched. The idea that a complete stranger could be watching their sexual prowess and jerking off while doing so, sent shivers down her spine.

"You're the most gorgeous woman I've ever met," he told her in a serious tone. His hands cupped her bountiful breasts. He loved the feel of her harden beads against his palms. He felt her body tremble. His cock twitched. He lowered his head and lapped her breasts with his tongue. He sucked hard on her nipples. His hands trailed down her ribcage and buried themselves between her thighs. His fingers teased her soft curls before gliding down the length of her slit, *oh so wet*, ready. He drove his finger deep inside of her.

"Please don't stop," she moaned.

He moved his finger inside with vigorous motion. He lowered himself in front of her without stopping the pumping action. His tongue dabbed her swollen clit. Her fingers dug through his hair and scalp. He loved the feel of her nails scratching him with need. He flicked his tongue back and forth on her clit; her wet pussy and getting wetter. He slipped in another finger with ease. Her muscles clenched around his knuckles in appreciation.

"More please give me more."

He drove another finger inside and suckled on her clit. Her pelvis arched against his mouth. He kept up the vigorous pumping. She bucked against him. Hot juices flowed over his fingers. He removed them in one quick motion and clapped his mouth over her lips, lapping up the squirting liquid.

Sydney's body turned into pure fire; never before had she experienced such a violent orgasm. The constant sucking pressure as he drank her juices brought her to the brink again as another intense wave of pleasure crashed over her. She felt her body go limp as it ebbed. Martial's hands squeezed her butt cheeks, his finger digging into her tender flesh lifting her as he stood up. He pressed her against the glass window, crushing her body with his. His mouth ravaged hers as he drove his thick cock deep inside her.

"You feel so good," he groaned, as he rocked his cock in and out of her pink folds.

Sydney clutched to his back, dragging her nails deep into his skin; sure she'd drawn blood, yet she couldn't stop. His long, hot cock plunging into her – hard and slow – hard enough that her butt cheeks were slamming against the cool translucent surface behind her. The thump, thump, thump of her ass echoed in her mind. It turned her on so much. She bit down on his earlobe.

Martial's insides had already been afire when her teeth clamped down on his earlobe now the inferno within exploded. He plunged into her again and again with wild abandonment. A savage cry tore out of him when he came like a beast filling her to the point of overflow.

Every nerve ending in Sydney's body alighted with heat. Heat that went beyond the simple fulfilling of a physical need, it warmed her through and through. She knew that her heart, her soul, belonged to him the moment his hot semen filled her womb. Her own orgasm had her flying. She bucked and ground against him and collapsed on his shoulders.

Martial tightened his hold on her and carried her across the sitting area into the bedroom and onto the king size bed where he laid her down gently.

"You are so beautiful and amazing," he whispered in her ear. She nuzzled her neck closer to his mouth. He pressed soft kisses on her moist skin.

With her buttocks pressed firmly against him and his arms securely wrapped around her, they fell asleep.

***

Sydney's fingers gripped the steering wheel so tight her knuckles turned white. Tears streamed down her face. She hiccuped and cried and screamed all at once. She'd fled from the cosy bed, and the man sleeping beneath the Egyptian cotton sheets, only minutes ago and she could feel the frost nipping away the heat. Little by little, it extinguished the fiery need that had consumed her earlier. When it reached her heart, it cracked; the pieces froze in her chest.

She'd affectively deceived the man she fell in love with. She swallowed the bitterness that filled her throat – how cliché of her to have fallen for him. Hook. Line. Sinker.

Can it really be called deceit if he'd never asked my name, she wondered. Bright, smart, are only two adjective linked to the man, he'd find Cassandra's bio in his press kit and he'd go to her, and he'd know right? That Cass didn't spend the night in his bed... in his arms. At least she hoped, that *he*, he would notice the differences between her and her best friend.

Would he ask Cass whom she sent in her stead? And even if he did would he care to meet the woman who duped him and then sneaked away? No, of course not. What man would?

Resigned, she stopped fighting the frosty feeling inside. She welcomed it. Basked in the numbness it provided. Sydney understood that her heart would remain in pieces. No other man could warm it again.

She reached across the passenger seat to grab the box of Kleenex she kept in the glove compartment. New tears flooded her eyes when she spotted the morning edition of the Ottawa Citizen that she'd automatically picked up in the lobby on her way out. The grainy black and white picture on the front page pulled her heart strings.

Someone *had* been watching – with telegraphic lenses too boot – the image showed her body draped over his. No mistaking what had taken place just before the lenses captured the shot. The head line read *Counsellor Gibbs finally shows his true hetero colors.* She flipped over the paper and backed out of the parking spot and drove away.

***

Martial woke with a start. His heart drummed in his chest. Tightness inside of him shook him to the core. He grasped for air, yet his lungs weren't filling up. Lights swirled in his head.

She disappeared!

He should have asked her to marry him when he'd cuddled her close to him. He'd been afraid it would have been too sudden. After all, he'd never even asked her name. In his mind an abundance of time remained; a lifetime lay before them to share those details.

Now, here stood wondering what went wrong.

Absentmindedly, he picked the heavy press kit from the chair. He flicked over the pages, scanning the head shots of the reporters that were covering last night's event. His heart stopped when his gaze settled on a pair of green eyes – Cassandra Waters.

One hour later, Martial walked out of the Hotel and made his way to the newspaper office.

***

While sitting at her desk, Cassandra finished the last edits on the story Sydney sent her when a man waltzed in the reporters den demanding to speak with her at once. She lifted her head in acknowledgment; giving her assistant the okay to send in him.

To her surprise, the man of the hour, Counsellor Martial Gibbs strolled in her cubicle.

"Counsellor Gibbs, to what do I owe this honour," she asked in a polite tone.

Martial's stomach fell to his knees. The voice sounded all wrong. The eyes looking back at him were a shade lighter and the lips were not as full. As if the evidence his eyes already drank in didn't provide enough, he let his gaze travelled down the young reporter's body. Wrong, all of it wrong: the swell of her breasts not as plentiful, her hips were slender – almost boyish, her legs, shapely, but missing a few inches. This woman did not equal his vixen! He couldn't find the words to ask this *Cassandra Waters* whom she'd sent in her place to the gala – whom at stolen his heart.

"Counsellor?" She said in a worried tone.

"I beg your pardon; I have you mistaken with someone else. I am so sorry."

Without further explanation, he turned on his heels and left her standing there with her jaw half open.

There'd be no happy ending for him, *yet*.

My Two Valentines

"Say it," Matt commanded.

I shook my head from side to side.

"Say it," he barked again.

I wrung my fingers and shook my head even more.

"Becca." His tone cold as ice made me give up my futile attempt and I admitted what he wanted to hear.

"Yes, I want you," I hated that my voice quaked so I filled my lungs once again and with composure I told him "But. I. Wont. Act. On. It." Each word precise leaving no room to mistake their intent. With that said I turned and walked away.

He overtook me after two steps.

"Becca." Now his voice turned into warm honey drizzling over my senses. I felt the sweetness of it melting away my resolve not to give in to him. I pulled up straight – spine rigid – shoulders squared. I looked up and up until I saw his deep brown eyes. "Matt," I felt proud that my voice remained detached.

"Let me have you," he purred.

"No." I side-stepped him and hurried down the hall to my apartment.

***

"Phhewwww." I exhaled the breath I hadn't realized I held onto. My encounters with Matt were getting more and more intense. I didn't know how long I would be able to hold him at bay.

Lip-smacking-scrumptious man any female would swoon over. Tall – 6'4" of sinuous muscles from head to toe, dark – tousled brown curls that I wanted to touch to see if they were as satiny as they looked, ruggedly handsome face – square jaw, slanted nose, lips – *oh my God can't think about those* – broad shoulders, powerful back, a waist that could actually be called one, long legs that looked good in anything. And a voice that filled me with ice cold shivers or searing hot need.

These feelings of mine they are just not normal at least not for Matt. *Off limits!* My mind screamed over and over again.

I couldn't help myself my fingers plucked at my cherry hard nipples through the soft material of my sweater and bra. I imagined his fingers there – circling, pinching, and teasing. My breath grew heavy. My eyes closed. My fingers continued to arouse me. In my mind I felt his mouth closing over my right nipple. My fingers added pressure there. I felt his tongue flicking over it. My fingernails scrapped the sensitive tip. My hips rolled. My head fell back against the closed door. "Mmmmmmmmm," a deep moan escaped from my throat.

Entrapped in my desire for him, I let my hands travel down my softly rounded stomach and reached low to grab my crotch. I squeezed it in my palm. My trousers were moist. I inhaled deeply. The strong musky smell of my arousal pushed me onwards in my fantasy. With dexterity that I didn't feel my fingers unbuckled my belt and unzipped my pants. They found my swollen clit. I bit on my bottom lip to stop myself from screaming out his name. I spread my legs apart and let my finger slip inside. "Mmmmm ahhhhhh," I moaned. I pictured him there, head between my open legs – licking, slurping, drinking – all the cream that oozed out. Another finger slid in the wetness.

My hips bucked against the door as I finger-fucked myself – quickly in – curving upwards reaching for that spot. "Mmmmmmmmmm ahhhhhhh," I cried out when they hit it. Two didn't give me enough. In entered a third – my teeth torture my bottom lip – could this be what it would feel like to have his tongue there. The thought drove me wild and my fingers grew wings. They flew in and out of my wet core. My inner walls constricted against my knuckles. My asshole squeezed a phantom cock. Hard and fast the muscles squeezed and squeezed. This time I couldn't stop it. "Yes, Matt, yes, mmmmmmmmmmmm," I screamed as my cream oozed out and down my thighs.

I floated somewhere in post erotic bliss. Eyes closed. Skin humming. A familiar voice grounded me back to my body when its muffled sound reached my ears through the door. "I heard that."

My eyes flew open. My cheeks became red hot. How could have been so careless. Of course he'd been standing there the whole time. Mortified I re-arranged my clothes and walked in my living room.

***

The next morning when I opened my door to leave for work a beautiful fiery red orchid lay taped to it with a little tag that said *Soon*.

Matt.

My heart somersaulted in my chest. I smiled and took the delicate flower inside. I loved that he didn't go for the obvious rose. *OFF LIMITS!* My mind screamed at me. My heart sunk back down. "Not fair," it whined.

The moment I opened the complex door the cold February wind nipped at my nose and cheeks turning them bright red. I made my way to work at a brisk pace. My face, fingers and toes were tremendously happy when I stepped in the heat of 'Silken Event's' main lobby.

"Good morning Miss Silk." Our receptionist greeted me.

"Hi S-Sandy." My lips chattered.

"Mr. Gerard would like to see you," she said with a look of apprehension in her eyes.

"Let him know that I'll be with him as soon as possible."

She wrung her hands. I arched my eyebrow and asked "What?"

"He said for you to go to his office as soon as you walked in." She pushed every word out slowly.

"Don't shoot the messenger, don't shoot the messenger," I told myself.

"Thank you, Sandy. Any other messages?"

"No, Miss Silk."

She still looked uncomfortable. "Hold my calls for a few hours, it appears I have a meeting," I said and wink.

"Will do, Miss Silk." Her tone took on its usual vivacity.

Still seething by the audacity of that man, I stomped away from the reception area and made my way to the large corner office. I banged the door opened and snarled at him "How dare you do that to Sandy, you prick bastard."

"Good morning, love." He ignored my outburst.

I slammed the door shut with the heel of my boot. Arms akimbo, feet planted in the plush carpeting, my eyes locked on his. "I. Am. Not. Your. Love." I said through clenched teeth.

"Of course you are, darling," he replied with confidence and threw me a wicked grin.

"Damn it Jess, when will you get it through your thick skull? We're not together anymore."

Jess Gerard, my ex-fiancé, looked me up and down with his penetrating green eyes. "You look... delicious."

My eyes rolled skywards showing my total exasperation. I had no doubt that he could also read the skepticism in them. They probably shone off a huge AS IF? Me. 5'3", short wavy locks of molasses for hair, eyes the color of green freckled mud, and more curves and contours than my small frame could take.

Well why not me?

Between Jess and his best friend, Matt Warner – my cheeks warmed at the thought of him- I swear though if they kept treating me like a delicious treat I might just start believing to be one. Shit! I hoped he didn't decipher that. I tore my gaze away from him. This so not the time to get off track, Jess knew which of my buttons to push to soften me up and use me like putty.

I drew in a deep breath and in an icy tone I told him "Get real Jess. And don't ever drag any other of the employees into this. Am I making myself clear?" I paused to make sure he got the message. "Now get the hell out of my office." I watched his tall frame squeeze through the door and couldn't help but smirk. At least he'd had the decency to realize that I wouldn't follow orders. With him out of the way I started my day.

***

Disappointment seeped through me when I didn't see Matt out in the hallway waiting for me. I sighed and dug out my key. Just as I turned the knob to open my door I felt him, near, watching me. Out of the corner of my eyes I checked the corridor to the right. Empty. To the left. *Bingo*. I saw him there in the shadows. A smile played on my lips as I entered my apartment. I closed the door and leaned my head against it.

For one so tall and muscular his footfalls were barely audible. I felt a charge through the door when he stopped in front of it. I held my breath, unsure of what he'd do next. Then I heard the sound of a zipper being pulled down. My heart raced. Every pore in my body wanted me to turn my head and watch him through the peep hole. I resisted the temptation and just listened.

At first I picked up the dripping kitchen faucet, the whirling furnace pushing in heat, the tick-tock of my grand-father clock. I pushed all these sounds aside and really concentrated on the man outside my door. I closed my eyes to enhance my hearing capacity. I heard him breath in and out in ragged pulls.

I heard the sound of skin moving over skin. I heard grunts and more heavy breathing. Slap. Slap. Slap. Slap. The rhythm went. Slap. Slap. Slap. Slap. Faster and faster. "Arrrrrrrrr." The sound of air being pushed through clenched teeth sent shivers down my spine. Slap. Slap. Slap. Slap. The breakneck rhythm continued.

I forgot how to breathe yet the sound of his arousal sustained me. His hands must have been moving incredibly fast over his cock and coming down hard on his thighs for the sound to be so intoxicating. The breathing on the other side of the door became as erratic as the tempo of the slap, slap, slap, and then the sweetest music reached my ears.

"Ahhhhhhhhhhhhhhhhhhhh."

My cheeky panties were soaked, my nipples rock hard and my pulse hammered I fanned my face with my hands.

"I know you heard that," he said and walked away.

**

The next morning another orchid lay on my door. This time its deep lavender color drew me in to drink in the exotic scent. I smiled and brought it inside. I cut the one word tag *Soon* and placed it in the island drawer with the first one.

All day long I went through the motions at the office – answering questions, extinguishing fires, restoring order here and there – even with all the tasks to occupy my hands, nothing captured my mind. It circled and circled.

"You busy sweetheart," Jess's voice and his use of the endearment grated like sandpaper on my skin.

"Yes I am. And stop calling me sweetheart or love or any other bloody things."

"Becca." His voice took on a serious tone. "When will you talk to me?"

I ignored the meaning of his words and remained professional, detached. "Jess, is there something I can do for you?"

He looked at me with a strange intensity. It took all my will power to remain calm and not to fidget under his scrutinizing stare. The effort exasperated me and the word blurted out of my mouth before I could stop it "What?"

His eyes danced over my body – caressing the generous swell of my breasts, devouring my softly rounded belly and curving hips. I felt like my clothes were being burnt away by his gaze leaving me exposed; vulnerable. His eyes smoldered. He stepped in closer. I put up my hands to stop him mid-track. "What?" I said again and gave myself a mental high five for the sharp clear voice. *No quivering here.*

Jess dragged his hands in his blond curls and exhaled loudly before answering "I miss you."

"Jess, I can't." I pulled in air deeply into my lungs.

"Soon," he whispered and left.

"Phewwwwwww," I exhaled my held-in breath.

My encounters with Jess were getting more and more intense. I knew that I would eventually have to address what happened between us, but now I didn't have the strength. Plus, I loved the ego boost it gave me to be chased by these two drop-dead gorgeous men.

The brutal walk home with its ice cold wind whipping at my coat and biting any exposed skin that by the time I rounded the last corner of the third block, I felt my body tremble from lack of heat. I put my head down to avoid the stinging wind as much as possible. In my haste to reach the door I didn't notice him blocking the way. I slammed into him and reeled backwards on my heels. His arms reached out and pulled me against him.

"Becca, you're frozen."

"H-ho-w n-ni-ni-ce o-o-of y-y-ou fo-r no-t-noti-n-otic-ing?" my teeth chattered.

"Let's get you inside."

He ushered me into the complex lobby and encircled his arms around me; too cold to stop him. I tried anyway. Feebly my arm pushed his away.

"Truce," he whispered in my hair. "You're as cold as a corpse and I am not into necrophilia."

My body shivered from the cold and the gruesome image that he'd burnt in my mind. He pulled me closer to him. I let his warmth radiate through me and leaned into him. We reached my door and he took my tote bag from me. I hid my growing grin in my scarf as I saw him rummage through the bag for my keys. With a triumphant look he pulled them out and unlocked my door.

"Go take a hot bath and get your body temperature back to its sizzling hotness. We can play tomorrow." He winked and walked away to his own door.

A pang of disappointment pierced through the cold. Too late, he had already gone in and closed his door.

***

As soon as my eyes fluttered open in the morning I jumped out of bed and rushed to the door. Sure enough another orchid awaited me. I squealed in delight and added it to my bouquet. My heart jumped and cart wheeled in my chest as my eyes and brain processed the tag note. Not just one word this time. Two words in beautiful script made my insides melt. *Be Mine.* I tucked the note in my bra and I left for work in a daze.

"Miss Silk, there's someone here to see you," Sandy said through my open doorway.

"Who?"

"Mr. Valentine."

I ran the name in my mental rolodex and came up blank.

"Show him in."

Sandy escorted a middle aged man with balding hair and protruding stomach in my office. First thought, this man should not be named Valentine.

"Miss Silk." His rich baritone voice however more than makes up for lack of appearance, and, made me re-think the unmatched name theory.

"Mr. Valentine." I rose and shook the offered hand. "What can I do for you?"

"I'm the new owner of Club Velour on York Street. I want to reopen it on Valentine's Day. I know that's one week from today. I've asked around Miss Silk, and they say you are the best. I want the best working on this."

The challenge of the insanely tight deadline might just be what I needed to keep my mind out of the gutter. "I will personally take charge of the event," I said with a radiant smile.

For the next hour we went over the details of the event and came up with a guest list. Two hours later the invitations, the menu and drinks were selected. More than three hours had passed by the time Mr. Valentine left my office. The building became quiet. I leaned back in my chair to go over the details for the Valentine event. I made notes, circled numbers and sent off a memo to our head of catering to order canapés and champagne. My eyes watered from the strain of working in the dim light. I closed the folder, shrugged on my jacket and pulled on my knee high boots.

The wind felt less intense on my skin this evening, my cheeks were just rosying up by the time I walked in the complex lobby. I made my way to my apartment. No Matt. My heart plummeted. I stopped in my tracks when I saw a box leaning on my door; the shiny black wrapping with a huge red velvety bow captured my immediate attention. With no visible tag that I could discern, I picked-up the rectangular gift and shook it gently. No sound. I unlocked my door and pushed it open. I placed the present on the glass table, took off my coat and shucked-off my boots.

Overwhelmed by curiosity I picked-up the box and brought it in my living room. I undid the bow and gently lifted the paper. Inch by inch I removed the satiny blackness to reveal more of it... the box all black shone just as much as the wrappings did. There were no markings on it. I turned it this way, that way; no names, initials, or any giveaways as to what may lie inside. I lifted the lid.

"Oh. My. God."

My fingers traced the delicate red Chinese silk scarves – all five of them – restraints for my wrists and ankles and one to use as a blindfold.

Matt?

Jess?

Something in the bottom left corner caught my eye. I picked-up the small black velvet pouch; it looked strangely familiar. My fingers pulled open the draw strings and reached inside to wrap around sleek cold metal. I took out the tube until in the palm of my hand sat a beautiful red lipstick vibe.

"Oh. My. God."

My pulse raced in my chest. My fingers played with the buttons and soon the little toy danced in my hand. My nipples hardened. My pussy moistened. Scarves forgotten I twirled the vibe between my fingers and ran it along my throat. The soft pulsing aroused my senses. I continued to move the magical toy lower towards my cleavage. I traced the contours of my omega breasts and let the vibe stimulate my nipples.

"Mmmmm, ahhhhh, mmmmmm," I moaned out loud as I moved the vibration down lower and lower until it dipped in my pants and found the my hard little nub. My hips rotated. My pelvis arched upwards to get more of the pulsing bliss given by this powerful lipstick. I bit my bottom lip, *hard*. My thumb pressed on the + sign and the toy danced on my clit – shock after erotic shock pulsed through me as I circled my clit with the vibrating delight. Unable to stop the orgasm from crashing, I let it consume me.

"Ahhhhhhhhhhh, yes, yes, ahhhhhhhhhhhhhh, yes," I screamed.

Depleted. Satisfied. I turned off my new toy. My limbs felt weak when I stood up.

I dropped the vibe like a hot potato when someone knocked on my door. In a disheveled sate I pulled open the door without even bothering to peep ahead. Matt looked at me with a knowing smile on his face "I see you enjoyed my present," his voice dripped like honey on my over sensitized skin. Oblivious to my frayed resolve, *huh no*, he knew what his voice did to me. He kept his tone soft, musical almost when he said "I received tremendous pleasure hearing you enjoying my gift. I look forward to using it on you myself – *soon*," his eyes burned with the lustful promises his words evoked.

"Matt..." He cut me off before I could say anything else. "For tonight, hearing your pleasure, while knowing I indirectly gave it to you, is enough. Well not quite." He bent his head down low, lower and found my lips. The contact although brief – *and oh so* – searing hot. By the time I opened my eyes again. He left.

***

The next morning a deep turquoise orchid lay on my door – strange – no tag. I brought it in and added it to my bouquet. Before going to work I stopped by my favorite bakery on Rideau Street to order the mini cream puffs, chocolate éclairs and the strawberry fourés. With that done I headed towards the flower shop and placed my order for the Club Velour reopening. Mr. Valentine had given me *carte blanche* in my selections; I avoided roses like the plague and went for orchids, freesias, dragon lilies and blood red spider flowers. Once again Sergio praised my choices and assured me that everything would be delivered promptly at 16h00 hours on February 14.

With Sandy being away from her desk when I walked in and I could have easily made my way to my office without any interruptions. Just to make sure though I checked the hallways – all clear – I hurried to my desk, pulled out the metallic red lipstick tube, capped it open and plugged it in the USB port. The little green charging light appeared. I exhaled and settled in to go through the planning lists.

Engrossed in my lists I didn't notice or hear Jess come in.

"Hey." His husky voice startled me.

With a hand clutching my chest to calm my racing heart I lifted up my head and found him there, a few inches away, his eyes glued to the red lipstick canister plugged in my computer. A smile played on his lips – like he knew the pun of the joke that had yet been shared.

"What?"

"Just came to see if you need help with anything. My own project closed down this morning and my new one is not due to begin until next week."

I knew the Velour reopening could use his entertainment savvy. I rummaged through my files and pulled out the one I wanted. "Here, you can take care of this," I said and handed him over the purple manila folder.

He quickly perused the outline and in neat block letters he made notes and comments. While his face remained intent on the file I felt at liberty to let my eyes explore his physique. His curls were as unruly as ever. His broad forehead creased in thought. His shapely eye brows slightly arched upward as his intense stare seem to be diverted to something in the file. His lips were full and sexy as sin. The dimple in the cleft of his chin where my tongue liked to lick... *Whoa, stop that thought.*

My eyes moved down quickly, taking in his slender frame. Everywhere they rested, my body remembered touching / tasting – the long column of his throat my tongue pushed against my teeth, the slim shoulders my fingers balled in my hands, the long almost to the point of gangly arms my arms felt empty, the lean torso and waist that dipped in a beautifully pronounced V with the help of his carved hip bones my nostrils flared. *Whoa, stop. Stop. Now.* With flaming red cheeks I pulled my eyes down to the gray speckled carpet. The drab color helped me get my running heart and libido in check.

"Becca?"

I lifted my face and watched his eyes search mine.

"What?"

"You looked, never mind, I'll get on this right away," he said instead.

"Thanks Jess."

His eyes looked past me and once again locked on the red lipstick.

"A gift?" he asked

Oh. My. God.

So many questions popped inside my head. Each of them abandoned before they could be finished. "How does he.." "Did Matt..." "Had Jess..." "Did they ..." "Would they..." through the consuming unraveling thoughts I must have shook my head in affirmative because Jess said "thoughtful of the sender," and winked before taking his leave.

As soon as his long trim legs were out the door I whipped the lipstick vibe out the USB port and dumped it in my tote bag. I spent the rest of the day in a state of disconnect.

***

When I arrived home my empty – gift less – corridor demoralized me even more. The next morning a new orchid – tag less. The day at work went by fast. With only days left before the reopening of Club Velour all of my energies were spent making sure this event succeeded. By six o'clock I considered myself almost ready to call it a night.

"You leaving Miss Silk," Sandy asked

"Soon."

"Okay then. Good night," she said and walked away.

I watched her leave the lobby and waited for her figure to pass by my office window before reaching in my tote bag. I pulled out one red silk scarf, the delicate material so soft on my skin made me tremble. I knew I shouldn't be doing this, yet I couldn't help myself. I brought the scarf to my face and wrapped it around my eyes. Blindly my fingers dug in my tote again and searched until they clasped the metallic tube. I pulled it out and hit the *on* button. The vibrations against my palm travelled down to my clit. Impatient, I brought the toy there.

"Ohhhhh, that feels incredible."

I didn't know if the fact that put on the blindfold increased the sensation or the one that I gave myself clitoris stimuli in my office, or maybe the combination of both played a part in it, but something made this feel way more intense than the first time I used the toy. My finger hit the + button again and again until I had it turned on full power. My hard swollen clit throbbed in unison with each vibration. "Ohhhh, ahhhh, mmmmm," I moaned and moaned.

So caught up in my desire to release the flood coursing through me, my ears didn't pick up the sound of feet being shuffled on the carpet or of breathes being pulled in and out in quick short gasps. They were only in tune to the quiet buzz of the vibe as it flew over my clit. "Ohhhhh, yess, yess, ahhhhh, yess, mmmmmmmmmmmmm," I groaned as hot cream gushed out of my pussy lips and trailed down my thighs. My breathing became heavy and erratic. The vein under my earlobe jumped with each thumping beat of my heart. My skin burned as if molten fire ran through my veins. Even if I just came, I didn't feel the happy release. I still felt tense and hungry for more. Frustrated, I turned off the toy and let it fall out of my hand.

In the ensuing silence the energy in the room change, it became electrified. My fingers reached for my blindfold. Strong masculine ones stopped me.

"Your best one yet," Matt purred.

His lips hovered over mine. His fingers traced the soft silk covering my eyes and dipped into my hair. I felt them tightening in the short locks as he tilted my head upwards. "You are so beautiful when you come," he whispered in my mouth before claiming it.

I relished the feel of his lips moving over mine. His tongue explored every hidden corner – licking tasting my inner cheeks, palate and tongue. My body completely tuned into his, that it didn't feel a second pair of hands working their way up my arms, shoulders, clavicles, down to my cleavage and back up the way they came. No, *it felt*, it just didn't register that the set of hands glued in my hair never moved from there. Matt slowed the kiss and gently released my locks. He grazed his teeth on my bottom lip before releasing me.

"Just beautiful," he whispered again.

I sighed.

"I have to go."

My heart plummeted at his words.

"Soon, you'll be mine."

I listened intently for the next few seconds. The room still felt charged. Like, like someone still lingered there. My fingers reached behind my head and unknotted the scarf. I blinked a few times to adjust my eyes and then I scanned the room – nothing – no one. Somehow I found the empty room deceiving. My body knew someone else had been here with Matt. It could only have been Jess. At that thought my heart ripped in two.

I broke off my engagement with Jess because I couldn't stop myself from wanting his best friend. No matter how much I loved Jess. No matter how good things were between us – *no matter how incredible the sex* – I found myself fantasizing about his best friend. When Fantasy didn't seem to be enough, when I began to look for a reason to brush up against him when we would all get together and I rescheduled my comings and goings just so I would cross him in the complex halls or lobby and my heart would skip a beat whenever he'd notice me... well

Christ, I nearly called out *his* name during... I knew my feelings ran deeper than just a simple crush. Just how deep those feelings ran I didn't want to find out. Utterly scared that I already knew the answer – I'd I fallen for Matt. I couldn't explain it. I loved Jess – the thought of hurting him – of betraying him, made my heart bleed. It didn't matter that I couldn't understand my feelings. He deserved someone that would love him completely and no one else. After that night of *nearly*, I walked away from Jess. Now here I sat six months later thinking that Matt and Jess were in cahoots together trying to seduce me, but to what end?

***

I spent the next few days in the same pattern: nocturnal arousal by sound – mine, his – come morning a new orchid, always a different color always tag less, left on my door. Until today – Valentine's day. I opened my door and found a huge bouquet of wild orchids and delicate freesias and exotic dragon lilies and perky spider flowers and a lone white tulip. On a blood red tag, written in beautiful script only one word that made my heart dance. *Tonight!*

Taking great care getting dress; I selected the perfect little black dress – the slinky one that hugged my generous cleavage and ruffled out and didn't cling to the rest of me. From my jewelry box I selected my knotted sterling silver tear drop necklace and matching earrings; applying a bit of make-up: mascara, liner, bronzer and lip gloss finished my look. I knew I should have worn the four inch silver heels, I also knew I'd be on my feet moving to and fro to ensure the success of this evening's event. Wisely, I left the heels behind and selected a flat sandal that crisscrossed on top of my feet and tied behind my ankles – sexy and comfortable. Dropping them in my tote bag I pulled on my boots.

Outside the sun up in sky shone bright. Despite the sun, the day still remained cold. At least this time no wind whipped at my coat or exposed skin. I hailed a cab and gave the driver the Club Velour address in the By Ward Market. The club bustled with activity. The catering crew finalized there set up and the bakery truck had just pulled-in with the sweet delivery. Sergio zipped this way and that leaving a trail of amazing flower creations in his path. Mr. Valentine stood behind the bar polishing the champagne flutes.

"Miss Silk, you have done a marvelous job getting this ready in such short notice," he said warmly.

"My outmost pleasure I assure you, Mr. Valentine."

"Becca," Jess's voice made my head whip around and the blood drained from my face when I saw Matt next to him. I glued my smile in place as they approached.

"Mr. Valentine, I would like to introduce Matt Warner, the best DJ in the National Capital Region. He's agreed to mix for your club this evening." Jess's smooth voice made the introduction.

Mr. Valentine remained momentarily speechless. He recovered after a few seconds and dropped the white rag he used to polish the glass and offered the DJ legend his hand. Matt took it and gave it a strong quick shake.

"Miss Silk, you've outdone yourself..."

"Mr. Gerard is our entertainment guru." I said and pointed my eyes at Jess "Give him your thanks to him. I'll circle around to make sure everything is set before the doors open."

"Thank you so much Mr. Gerard." I heard him say as I walked away from the bar.

The table cloths were white on white. Long snowy white tapers sat in the middle of each table. Sergio's flower arrangements added a punch of color here and there. Only one table, in the nook at the back, near the DJ booth stood out amongst the rest. The table cloths were black on black. A long silver taper sat in the middle and nearly a dozen white tulips lay in a scattered bundle next to it. I looked around to see if I could spot Sergio anywhere. I couldn't d find him. I moved closer to the table and stopped in my tracks when I heard Matt and Jess approaching. I pivoted on my heels and changed direction. Once I'd circled the room and assured myself that everything ran in orderly fashion I made my way back to Mr. Valentine.

"Are you ready?"

"Yes."

"The honor is yours."

I let him step out from behind the bar and watched him make is way to the entrance glass doors. He pushed them opened to let the eager guests come in out of the cold. And so the night began. Matt's music choices were elegant and classy as much as they were fun and flirtatious. Soon couples were twirling on the dance floor. The food flew out of the kitchen and the champagne flowed.

"Here, you look like you could use this," Jess said as he handed me a bottle of water. He knew, like all my employees, no one drank on the job.

"Thanks," I said and capped it open to take a deep long pull. I felt his eyes on me the whole time. "What?" I asked after putting the bottle down.

"Have I told you today how beautiful you are?"

Nervous laughter bubbled out of me and somehow through it I manage to say "No."

"Let me rectify that. Becca, you're so beautiful."

My cheeks warmed.

"Especially when you blush."

This of course only made my cheek flush even more. "Jess, quit it." I said without any real conviction.

"No, Becca, you really are beautiful," he repeated as he stepped closer to me. Not fast enough to put up my walls up in time; his next words left me breathless "Gorgeous. Perfect. Mine." Next thing I knew his arms were around me; his mouth came down on mine. My arms locked around him. My mouth ravaged his. In this familiar embrace, I felt the *all consuming love* I had for this man resurfaced. How did walk away from this?

"Sorry, I didn't mean to interrupt." Matt's voice pulled me out my bliss-with-Jess bubble. The timbre of it melted my insides. The naked lust in his eyes made my heart race in my chest. This is how I walked away from it. These insane pullings and wantings snipping away pieces of my heart, storing them for the day they could be given to him. I didn't trust my voice so I remained silent.

"No worries," Jess said in a carefree way and then added, "is it time?"

Matt nodded.

Jess's smile spread wickedly across his face. He leaned in to me, gave me a quick hot kiss, pivoted and walked away.

What could that man be up to?

I turned to face Matt. His deep brown eyes were soft and honest. In them shone a deep rooted lust and, *God help me*, love. At this point I felt damn sure he could read the confusion and the lust and, yes the love, in mine as well. A smile played on his lips. His fingers reached out to trace my jaw from earlobe to chin. His digit ignited tiny fire bursts of desire. Desire that spread everywhere.

"Ladies and gentleman may I have your attention please." Jess's clear voice reached every corner of the room. He waited for the guests to settle and for silence to descend before continuing.

"On this Valentine's evening I would like to share with you a tale of hearts.

Once, not so long ago, a man met a beautiful, intelligent, funny woman. It's no wonder that the man fell madly in love with the exquisite creature. To his extreme surprise she loved him too. They shared each other's hopes, dreams, and life aspirations.

One day about a year after they met, in a nervous flutter the man got down on his knees, pulled out a ring and asked her to marry him – astonished and proud – on cloud nine like totally elated when she said yes.

Alas, he fell from cloud nine when he noticed his love pulling away from him. She became reserved and introspective. He felt something troubling her – new feelings taking roots in her core.

He couldn't be jealous because he knew he held in his hands a rare jewel. So no, he couldn't be jealous that others wanted her. Petrified of losing her love, yes that emotion gnawed at him more then he wanted to admit. But he felt it every day – in her smile, her touch, her kiss – he felt her love for him still as strong.

Yet, he could see a new love begin to form.

Oh. What to do?

He could think of nothing to ease this pain from her heart. When she walked away he watched in complete dismay. The light in his head exploded – showed him how deep his love ran, how it could conquer everything. This knowledge opened new and unconventional possibilities. He didn't care about society and politically correct. He wants her; she wants him, and another. That's okay. She can have that. So on this Valentine's night, I am here to say, to my love – be mine, be his, be ours – we'll love you forever. Please say yes and put my heart, his heart, your heart, out of misery."

Tears streamed down my cheeks. This couldn't be. Everything felt surreal. I didn't notice him step down from the podium and make his way towards me, didn't even feel my legs anymore. Vision blurry I stumbled; he caught me. Here stood one of my heart's pillars. I turned and found the other standing there supporting me as well. For the first time in long time I felt my heart whole in my chest. In a choked whisper I said "yes."

Two sets of digits squeezed my hands. We pulled apart before any of the other guests noticed us huddled together. Jess mingled around the room. Matt went back to the DJ booth. I made my way to ladies rooms to fix my make-up. With a fresh face I re-joined the party, checked on the desserts being brought out, ensured that the last of the champagne flowed. Mr. Valentine motioned me from behind the bar. I crossed over to him.

"Miss. Silk, thank you so much. This surpasses all of my expectations. I have feeling that after tonight this club will bloom."

"Mr. Valentine, your club is beautiful, clean and chic. That by itself brings in clients. Tonight, we only showcased the great values you already have in place. I agree with you this place will thrive." I smiled and shook is offered hand.

"Miss. Silk it's been a pleasure working with you, and I am sure I'll be calling you soon."

"I look forward to it Mr. Valentine."

Matt announced the last song of the evening. A sultry rendition of Frank's Sinatra *The way you look tonight.* I had no doubt that he selected that song for me; his eyes devoured my silhouette as I made my way towards the black on black table. I reached out and traced the contours of each tulip. The soft petals cool on my fingertips. Eleven white tulips were loosely bundled together. I knew the twelfth one had been left in the bouquet outside my door that morning.

Tears sprung in my eyes again, I blinked them away. When the last of guest left, the catering truck idled at the loading doors while the last of the crates where being carried in and the staff walked out the door I felt a strange sense of impatience wash over me. Anxious for what would happen next. Jess told a great tale, in reality could this work? My heart hammered in my chest in anticipation – ready to find out.

"They're for you." Matt's sweet tone ringed in my ear.

"I know." I said and picked up the white tulips.

"We're taking you home."

"I know."

Overheated by the turn of events I couldn't bring myself to slip on my coat and by looking at them neither could they. I draped mine over my arm as we walked out into the snow. I didn't feel the cold, the heat infusing me radiated through and through. My body grew tenser and tenser. The drive home felt way too short. The energy in the small confine space of the vehicle pressed on my nerves and pulsed through my core. The cold night air helped to decrease some of the pressure but my body still felt charged. We made our way inside the complex hand in hand. It intoxicated me to be strolling along on the arms of these men – *my men* – wow. It would take some time for that concept to fully sink in.

When we reached my door, Jess's free hand took my tote bag and dove to the bottom to pull out my keys. He passed them to Matt to unlock the door. As soon as we crossed the threshold, my coat hit the floor. Lips claimed me, arms encircled and lifted and squeezed me between two fabulous male torsos. I felt the ridges of hard cocks on my thighs and butt. Hands moved up my arms and pulled down the straps of my dress, it slipped between our pressed together bodies and pooled at our feet leaving me in my underwire balconnette bra, my cheeky panties and thigh high socks. Lips ravaged mine. My hands locked in satiny brown curls *even better than I'd imagined.* My back arched pushing my breasts onto the opened palms cupping them. "Mmmmm," I moaned.

Busy fingers were working the hooks of my bra, when the last one came free the cups were peeled off me. New fingers kneaded my breasts, pinched my nipples. My legs wrapped around a waist. My fingers pulled the brown curls up; lifting his face away from my lips and pushing it downwards to my erect nipples. Jess's hands were traveling up and down my spine. His lips left a trail of sloppy open-mouthed kisses on the back of my neck and shoulder blades.

"Mmmmmmm, ahhhhhhhh, ohhhhhhhhh," I groaned when Matt's lips close over my right nipple. His tongue flicked to and fro. Jess's teeth grazed the sensitive skin at the base of my skull and his fingers worked in slow sensuous circles lower and lower down until they reach my ass crack.

Matt's hands moved up my thighs, fingers slipped under the elastic of one of my thigh high black sheer sock and rolled it down delighting in each new section of exposed skin. They repeated the slow sensual process with my other leg. When I stood there with only my panties on his eyes roamed over my bare curves and heated up. The intensity of his desire burned deep – unmistakable. His fingers were eager on my skin as they moved down the lumps of my rounded belly and reach the top of the lacy cheekies they dipped under the soft material to find my pulsing clit. I bit on my bottom lip and grounded my pelvis against him.

Jess's pulled me back towards him and skimmed his own fingers over my barely covered asshole. "I hope you're not fond of this pair, love," he said as his fingers tore them off me. "Oh, you are so sexy." His voice held a note of reverence that melted my core. Here I stood nude before my lovers and they were both looking at me with fire in their eyes as if I truly could be the best looking thing they'd ever seen. They're eyes shone with such love and longing I could no longer deny what they'd been telling me all along... me Becca Silk equaled beautiful – no matter the extra curves I carried – I actually equaled beautiful. Tears pricked the back of my eyes, I blinked them back. Even if they would have been happy tears I didn't want them to spoil this moment. Impatient to get his hands on me Jess grabbed my ass and teased my puckered opening pressing it together, pulling it open squeezing my butt cheeks tight and releasing them quickly. Matt's thumb circled my clit and his long index finger slipped inside my wetness "Mmmmmm, yess, mmmmmm, yesss," I screamed as the orgasm crashed over me.

Jess's finger joined Matt's. They both moved in and out of my slippery pussy lips. With a well lubricated finger Jess played with my asshole slowly pushing it in and out and in deeper until he had it buried to his knuckle. The sensation of Jess's digit in my ass and Matt's in my pussy felt incredible and I couldn't wait for their cocks to fill me that way. I thrashed against them bucking my hips outward to bump one cock and inwards to hit the other one. Matt's mouth touched me everywhere – kissing, licking, and slurping. His finger slipped out my pussy and reached for his zipper. He leaned my body back against Jess, aligned his cock to my wet entrance, braced his legs and plunged in. "Ohhhhh, mmmmmmmm, ahhhhh," I moaned.

Jess rocked me forward impaling me more on Matt's cock. I heard another zipper being pulled down. Jess bent me a bit more forward. I felt his bulbous head opening my asshole. Matt stayed still inside of me as my ass took in Jess's shaft an inch at a time. Fingers did not give this feeling justice. The thin membrane of skin separating the erections of my lovers as they moved in perfect rhythm in and out of me... well I have no words to describe how it felt... all I can say is that I never wanted them to stop. Matt pushed in. Jess pulled out. Matt pulled out. Jess pushed in. Lips claimed mine. Lips licked and tasted my back. Fingers plucked at my nipples. Fingers found my clit and rubbed it. My body actually experienced a sensation overload. The orgasm raging through me too intense for any coherent words I screamed out "Mmmmm, yess, yess. Mmmmm. Matt. Jess. Mmmm. Yess. God. Jess. Matt," as hot cream gushed out of me.

The rhythm changed pace. Their cocks pounded my pussy and ass faster, harder and deeper. I felt like I would be ripped open from the intensity of their pounding. Another orgasm built, I focused on their hard heavy grunts. I grounded my hips rocking their cocks inside me as my muscles squeezed and squeezed the long hard thick shafts filling me.

"Arrrrrrrr ahhhhhhhhhhhhhhhh," they both groaned as their semen shot out and overflowed my pussy and dripped down my ass and thighs.

Jess leaned his head forward, nipped my ear and whispers "I love you, Becca."

Matt bent down his head and before claiming my lips in searing kiss he said "I love you, Becca."

Matt's lips released mine. I looked him in the eyes and said "I love you, Matt." I turned my head and locked my eyes on Jess "I love you, Jess."

In my heart I knew this would work.

Hidden Talents

Hide and Seek

"I saw that."

"What?" My voice is thick and sweet. My husband is not buying my innocent act for a minute. His left eyebrow arch into his hairline and his gruff whisper tingles on my skin.

"That."

"Oh, you mean this." I flick open the long skirt of my evening gown to reveal manicured fingers disappearing within the glistening pink folds of my bare pussy. His breath catches in his throat, his eyes turn opaque and his nostrils flare. On pure animalistic instinct his tongue darts out of his mouth and rolls across his lower lip.

"You look parched."

"I am."

I slide my sandals off my feet and bring them up close to my butt cheeks on the plush upholster seat. I lift my lower limbs off the rich fabric arch my back and reach backwards with my arms to grab the empty seat behind me. I love that I am flexible enough to offer him up my pussy as if on a platter. As soon as I stop wiggling into position his face is between my legs, nose running the length of my drenched slit inhaling every ounce of my arousal.

"You smell so good." His warm breath sets off a series of tiny bursts. The intense heat they provide has me gasping. My inner walls clench around phantom fingers. Sensing my impatient need his tongue slides out of his mouth and runs along my puffy lips.

Espionage

"George, what are you looking at? The stage is over there." My wife's nasally whisper grates on my already frayed nerves. *I know the stage is over there, but right there in the third box to the left of the stage a woman is getting her pussy eaten out and my cock is swollen to the size of a freakish zucchini in my pants. Of course I can't tell her that. Not Miss Sunday Night with all the lights off doing the missionary without any fast or sudden thrusts.* To view such a display would be most offensive to her. Without a doubt she'd have the enticing couple thrown out of the opera house. I shift in my seat to relief the pressure my growing cock is causing and turn towards her.

"My apologies, I dozed off." The lie rolls off my tongue with practiced ease.

"George." Her tone is full of reproach. In her eyes only a simpleton would ever dare fall asleep at a representation of **Carmen**. Her eyes remain frozen on me until I shift my regard towards the stage. I long to see what *they're* doing, but she does not trust my ability to remain focused on the production. In a small rebuke of my own I lean into her and whisper "Madam, you're missing the act." The rustle of silk on upholstery tells me she shifted in her seat to better view the scene.

I keep my eyes on the production until I am sure she's absorbed in it and turn my greedy eyes towards the third box to the left. *Oh god, that pussy looks delectable. The way he flicks and twirls his tongue across her swollen pink button makes my mouth water for a taste of the juicy morsel.* My cock expands even more. The pressure of my engorged head pushing against the zipper of my slacks is barely tolerable.

This, of course, is my punishment for going commando. I hate wearing this monkey suit she dresses me in. Leaving the "boys" some breathing room is my way to defy my prim and proper wife.

"George. Honestly. Wake-up."

I jump at her irate tone and fix my gaze on the stage until the curtain drops announcing the intermission. Just as the curtain touches the floor I chance a glance in the third box to the left. I glimpse a swish of skirt exiting the private entrance. A sigh escapes my lips.

"Oh, show some respect George!" she says in her most exasperated tone yet.

"Of course my dear." I stand, tug and readjust my pants before offering her my arm to guide her out of our own box.

Telling the future

The line-up for the ladies room is long as always in situation like these. I don't really mind. I just had a mind blowing orgasm. The fact that my thighs are slick and creamy is well hidden underneath the heavy skirts of my gown. I enjoy pressing them together. The squish, squish sound the friction makes gets me hot all over again.

Finally there's an opening. I enter the large stall. I grab moist toilettes from my hand bag and proceed to clean up my thighs and swollen pussy lips. I can't help but graze my red hot clit. It throbs beneath my fingertip. My nipples pucker. I arch my chest to rub them hard against the boning of my bustier. A moan floats out of me. And my finger is off. Vigorously massaging, rolling, and pressing my clit so hard, I cry out in ecstasy when a new flood of juices gushes out of me.

"What are those awful noises?" I hear a nasally pitch voice exclaim.

I clamp my fingers to my mouth, biting down on them as I ride out the last of my orgasm. As clean myself up for a second time a soft giggle escapes my lips. Whoever spoke, it sure seemed like she needs to ride a good long one. It would probably remove the stick up her butt that causes her voice to reach near screech levels. With a radiant smile on my face I exit the stall and wash my hands in the now deserted restroom.

Meet anyone lately?

"George, you'll never believe what I think I heard in the women's lavatory."

I really don't want to know what she thinks she heard, but I play along and gaze down on her immaculate features with an expectant look splashed across my face.

"I think a woman..." she discreetly turns her head this way and that and lowers her voice even more before continuing "touched," she gulped "I mean coupled" again her eyes dart left and right to make sure no ears are within our circle and says "with herself." Her face is beet red at her confession.

My now subdued cock wakes up in earnest at her words. It stands erect and pushes uncomfortably against my zipper. *Not again.* I rotate my hips in the hopes of relieving some of the pressure. I stayed silent too long when I see my wife's mouth turn into a pout and the petulant words "you don't believe me," hiss out of her crooked lips.

"Of course I do. Only thing is what appropriate reply did you wish me to make dear?"

I see her pondering my question until finally in a resigned tone she says "you are right George, there's no appropriate reply for you here."

I smile and gently pat her hand "Why don't you go back in and I'll bring our drinks."

"Champagne. Very chilled. Very Crisp."

"I know." It takes every ounce of my willpower not to roll my eyes at her. My stomach tightens in hope as I watch her trim figure make its way towards our box and turn to wait in line to order our drinks. *Damn that woman could be so hot, if it wouldn't be for the huge stick up her toned little behind.* When I turn I collide against a hard frame. Stunned, is the only expression that could describe my facial features, because here is the man I've been spying on for most the night and I just spilled his drinks all over myself.

Flustered, I hammer out a lame apology in guttural grunts. The man smiles warmly and waves off my apology. "Here let me help you." My eyes close when the smell of his tangy breath hits my face. There's a bit of sweetness to the tang. *Damn I knew that pussy looked delicious.* In a start, I bring myself out of my daze only to be plunged into another one. My feet stay glued in place as I watch in disbelief at the stranger kneeling before me while patting down my drenched slacks.

I am mortified when my cock swells.

Air leaves my lungs as the stranger's head moves up and closes in on my crotch. His nose bumps my rigid shaft. He chuckles and straightens up. "Please, join me and my wife in our private box and we can take care of the rest of you."

Tasty Treats

I watch my husband escort a man into our box. I give him the once over. He's cute. Tall with dirty blond curls flopping in his chocolate brown eyes. He's lean but his well cut suit shows off the sinuous and taut muscles of his chest and legs. I almost smack my lips together when my sight takes in the long hard bulge of his crotch. MMMM. What a treat.

"Honey, this is George."

His hand is warm and firm in my palm when he shakes my hand. I like that. Confidence is such a lethal aphrodisiac. I feel the moisture build. My breathing shallows. My pupils dilate. My husband, astute as ever, picks up on my signals and knows I am ready for another round.

"I thought we could help him relieve some of the pressure he's under."

"Oh, I am sure we can." I wink at George and without any preamble I flick open my skirt and let the men get drunk on the essence of my arousal.

Bewildered, George drops to his knees. He inhales deeply and lets his eyes close in a moment of serenity. Mimicking him, I close my own eyes and let myself be swayed by the sensual energy he discharges. I relish the feel of his hands as they skim over my bare calves and move up. There's nothing more alluring to me then to make a confident man loose it a little. I want to dance with erotic glee when I feel his hands tremble against my limbs. With fear, excitement or need I don't know. All of the above I suspect. The higher they reach the more they shake and the more they shake the more aroused I become. My pussy creams and tightens in anticipation.

George pauses when his thumbs move up my knees. In encouragement I part my legs even more giving him full access. His fingers dig in my tender flesh and his tongue laps up my dripping slit.

"Ohhhhhhhhhhhh," I let out a long moan and my fingers dive into his silky hair. His tongue takes it sweet time licking me up and down. Careful to avoid tickling my hard little nub the tip of its impressive length plunges inside my open lips. "Ahhhhhhhhhhhhhh," another moan floats out of my throat.

I sense my husband's energy before I feel him kneel between us. He's nearly belly on the floor, neck arched like a swan; it's the only way for him to accommodate his long frame and still partake in these erotic delights. I knew he wouldn't be able to stay away from George's rock hard erection. I hear a zipper being pulled down. Followed by two hard gulps – my husband's in pure pleasure of the treat he's about to devour and George, in both disbelief and shock that he's not repulsed by a man cupping his tomato sized balls.

The sucking and slurping noises of my husband's mouth moving down George's shaft combined with George's own drinking and gulping of my intense flood makes my heart race. I feel like a hundred wild mustangs are stampeding inside my chest where my heart used to be.

Prim and proper unleashed

Where is that man? I swear even with the simplest instructions he still gets lost. Dozing off at the opera, to **Carmen** *no less, I hope he's not sleeping in the lobby. No. He wouldn't embarrass me like that. Maybe he got turned around and went in the wrong box. Oh, I hate missing the piece, but there's no helping it. I'll only peek at the other boxes and see if I can spot him.*

This is useless. I don't see him anywhere. Only five boxes left. No. No. Ohhh. Ohhh. Ohhh. That's. Well that's. Ohhh. Ohhh. Ohhh. Is it hot in here? No; it's me. I am hot. REALLY HOT. Tingly even. If I squeeze my legs really tight maybe that'll help. I never knew he could do that. Ohhh. Oh, George. If only I knew...

Without being conscious of it, my body is upright and my feet are guiding me out of our private box. In a daze, I make my way towards George and his amazing tongue. I feel my pussy clench in my French silk panties. They're moist. They've never been moist. My nipples feel like swollen blueberries ready to explode. Oh God, they hurt.

The groans and moans emanating from the luxurious box propel me to move inside its threshold. With the Opera glasses I didn't spot the man on his knees sucking my husband's cock so I am taking aback by the sight of him. Yet, I've never seen George's erection this hard or this long or well, this big. I should be revolted by the scene. I'm not. I am aroused. And yes, jealous that I'm not the one who made him this-this crazy.

"Oh. Oh. Oh. Oh." The husky moans and shallow breathing from the unknown beauty takes my attention away from my husband's member and onto where his busy mouth is.

His long large tongue is plunging in and out of another woman's pussy. His thumb is pressed hard against her clit. Her legs shake from the pleasure she's receiving. Her pussy is creaming up beautifully. The powerful smell of her muskiness invades my nostrils. I can't help but breathe it in deep. I'm surprised to find that my own arousal mixes in with hers. My panties are now completely wet.

I reach behind my back and tug down the zipper of my gown. I let it pull at my feet. I cup my breasts through the soft material of my bra, my overripe nipples burn under my fingertips. I push down the cups and the gentle whoosh of cold air hitting them makes my breath intake sharply. I bit my bottom lip in fear that my presence would be announced. None of the others seem to have heard my hard intake of air. Relieved, I move my hands down my lean torso and continue south until my fingers slip under the elastic of my panties. I slide them down my legs to the grown and step out of my dress.

Naked, I kneel next to the strange man sucking my husband's cock. I watch his technique for a few minutes. The way his cheeks concave, his lips pucker out, how his throat muscles relaxes as George's exciting length pushes further down. WOW. It seems like George's cock will reach this man's navel the way it keeps going down and down. *Can I do that?* I take a deep breath and lean in closer. I have to give it to this stranger. He didn't start or anything. He simply moved his head aside and let me have a go at my husband's pulsing cock.

I feel his heated gaze take in my naked form. I smile at him in invitation and suck on the engorged head greedily. The fact that it jumps in response, encourages me to suck it even more. *Oh, my. This feels good*: hard and soft, veiny and pulsing, alive inside of me. I silently congratulate myself for not jumping out of my skin when new hands cup my sensitive breasts.

I moan around a mouthful of cock encouraging my illicit lover to continue. His thumb and forefinger closes over my stiff nipples. In an excited shiver my teeth grazes the velvety skin. This action sets off a wild fire in George. His fingers twist my pixie locks and his pelvis rocks forward. Somehow I manage not to gag when his mushroom head tickle my tonsils. I almost choke when a scorching tongue flicks my left nipple. When it's sucked inside an inferno, I bite down the steel rod greedily pumping down my throat.

The events that followed are a blur. Sensation overload if you will. All of the sudden, strange fingers were moving inside my own wetness. Fast and furious they touched, caressed my inner walls and pressed hard against my G-Spot. This invasion has me breathless. Add the fact that George's cock grows even harder and larger inside my mouth. I feel light headed and dizzy. Drunk actually. Yes, I am drunk on the overwhelming power I feel.

This is my mouth on him. Making him this aroused; this crazy. Frantic, bordering on desperate are the only words I can think of to describe the way his erection propels within the suction my mouth provides. I am doing this to him. My husband, George, the man I believed to be a polite lover. Perhaps I am responsible for that, I've been brought up to believe that intercourse is a sullied thing to be endured in order to procreate.

Procreate, I cannot do. My ovaries are fatigued my gynecologist tells me. I can do drug therapy to zing them up a little, but the side effects are wicked and the chances are minimal. George and I agreed not do it. Since I can't produce any offspring, our coupling has been routine. Boring. I've often fantasized about George taking me, upright plastered against the wall with wild desperate need. Or of me, seducing him in the middle of the afternoon by walking in his study completely naked demanding to be pleasured. Many a nights those fantasies have given me chills. This is so much better than fantasy.

To feel. To touch. To taste. So pure a desire is electrifying. My skin sizzles. I am sure the stranger fingering me feels it. I don't care. I am liberated. I concave my cheek deeper, creating a vacuum with my lips. I suck harder. I am rewarded with heavy grunts and limbs trembling. Behind me I am aware of other limbs quaking. She's close. I'm close.

I feel it raging in my belly. My most intimate muscles clench and release around protruding knuckles. In response to my squeeze his mouth sucks in my nipple deeper inside the inferno. His tongue swirls around it. In a loud pop the abused appendage is released. In what feels like reverence, his hands gently cup my breasts. In slow motion digits skim the sensitive wet tip. His head bends down anew and my right breast receives the same delicious treatment.

Explosion

The pungent smell of orange blossom drifting in the seaside air wafts over me. A new player has joined our little group. I crack open my eye. The delicate beauty now sucking George's cock reminds me an oversized fairy. She's tall, slim and curvy in all the right places. My husband is getting a mouth full of her breasts. They're like swollen grapefruits with fat plump raisins protruding out of them.

Unlike my husband I am not bisexual, but I can honestly appreciate the female form in all its beauty. And this creature kneeling, crouching between my legs is stunning. Her skin is all peaches and creams. Her hair is cut very short. Very chic. All spikes and twirls. I like how it showcases her high cheek bones, the daintiness of her brow and the sharp line of her nose. Her lips are puckered out and look juicy with a huge cock ramming in and out of them.

If this is George's wife then I don't understand why his large flat tongue is massaging my pussy walls instead of hers. She's a vixen. "A real sex on legs kind of gal." Yet, I can't feel sorry about how the events of the night have turned out.

George's tongue is exquisite. "OHH. OHHH." Especially when he folds it like that and spears it in and out. "Ohhh. Ohhh. Yes, again. Do it again." My breathless command is not lost on him. His folded tongue repeatedly lances in. I feel all my muscles clench at once. I am ball of tension. This feeling of increase tightness drives me crazy. Just when I think I can't take it anymore George's thumb presses against my clit and the tip of his tongue unrolls against my sweet spot.

Everything inside of me releases. Like an elastic band let loose to fly. Yes, I am flying high. Euphoric energy fills the room as the others soon follow me over the edge of sanity. For a few long breath catching minutes everyone is in their own blissful bubble. Little by little reality sets in.

"Candice?" The astonishment in George's voice barely covers the culpability vibe of *busted*.

"Oh, George, you were wonderful."

"What?"

I believe that George's confusion mixed with a genuine guilty air helps his cause.

"Oh, George. I'm so sorry. I've been so uptight for so long. I never knew."

"Candice. I...I don't know what to say. I..."

"I think introductions are in order."

Flustered, George shakes his now limp penis inside his slacks and zips up. He introduces us to his wife and she smiles warmly at my husband. I love how she carefully mouths the words "thank you" at him behind her hand. I am sure George saw it as well. If he did, he didn't let it show. I am sure that all in all he's still pretty perplexed that his straying has led to this happy conclusion.

"George, Candice, it has given us great pleasure to have met you both this evening. Would you do us the honor of becoming our box buddy's?" My husband's rich baritone tickles my senses. Heat rises once more inside me. I am astonished at my own libido. I am so ready to fuck him. I turn my lustful gaze at him and he returns a loaded one at me. Oh my. I want out of here. Now. I re-attach my skirt to my bustier and twirl about.

"You look lovely." I take his arm and let him escort me out.

Revelation

"Candice?"

Alone in the luxurious suite I turn and face George. He's tense. His brow is beaded with sweat. His fists are scrunched like tennis balls. I slide over to his side, lean into his frame and whisper in his ear. "Let's go home George. I want your tongue to do those wonderful things to me."

I step over my dress and make it to the threshold before George realizes that I am in my undergarments, "Candice, your dress."

"My prison you would mean."

He's confused by my words.

"George, tonight, for the first time I feel free. No, it's more than that. I feel like a woman. Silly, I know. I am a woman I should feel like one all the time. But I never do. I always repress and shy away from my sexuality. No more. From now I'm me."

In giddy excitement I twirl on my tiptoes and throw my arms up in the air. He shrugs off his suit jacket and wraps it around my shoulders. I am not in the least bit embarrassed that I am walking out into the Opera House showing off my new wantonness. I giggle at the momentary upraised eyebrows and the slight smirk on the usher's face as I pass by.

Who knew I could be such an exhibitionist.

This Christmas I will...

December 12

Juls,

Everyone is acting crazy. This the season to be jolly – *not crazy*. But the crazies must be catching, because I am suddenly feeling like I can't spend another Christmas without telling... I need him – and by him – I mean Max.

Yes, Max Abraham.

I need him to notice me. Like, really see me. I want him to want me. I *need* him to want me. I need him to rip my clothes off. I need him to touch me everywhere with his eyes, his hands, his lips, and his body. Christ, I need him to fuck me until I don't know my own name. And when I remember my name, I want him to make love to me so slowly, so thoroughly that I'll forget it all over again.

I am nuts.

Of course I am nuts – I am planning to seduce my best friend here.

Juls, please, I need your help. Guide me in this crazy seduction plan of mine.

Who am I kidding?

If you were still here – *God, I miss you Juls* – you'd be the first one to tell me not to do this. Wouldn't you? I just can't keep up this façade of mine for another Christmas. I need him to know. Know how I really feel. How I've felt all along. Okay, *maybe not all along*, but it seems that way to me.

We were thirteen, getting ready for our elementary grad/prom shin-ding. When I looked at Max that night, the butterflies settled in my stomach. Throughout high school I watched him from the sideline, hardly able to keep the butterflies from suffocating me. College came and went; me at one end of the country, him on the other even complete opposition did nothing to calm the swarm of butterflies.

Remember Grams used to tell us that time could fix all sorrows. Well not even time could get these butterflies of mine to flutter away. I've grown accustomed to them... Heck I've lived with them for nearly twenty years! I accepted that they're here to stay. Stay, that is until I give them what they want. What I want.

A taste of Max. All of Max. Forever.

No, no. I can't do this. I can't put my feelings out there. I am scared Juls and I don't want to spend another Christmas wishing he could be mine. Is this the craziest thing I've ever attempted? If I ever tried to do anything crazier I don't remember.

You'd remember.

I wonder if you knew – about Max – how I felt. Did you know Juls?

Guess I'll never know.

Miss you like crazy.
xox

Paying no attention to the gush of cold air that hit her face as she closed her journal of morning pages, Myriam Volterre put it away in the drawer of her bedside table. Ready to face the day, she got out of bed and headed for the kitchen to start the coffee. It didn't take long for the rich velvety aroma of her favorite Peruvian blend to fill the air and wake-up her taste buds.

With a brimming cup of coffee in one hand and half a toasted bagel in the other she headed towards her tower; a semi-circle room at the back of the house. Its large oak staircase that climbed up to the second storey gleamed in the early morning light. The bottom part she reserved as her office space: desk, chair, laptop, printer, pads, pens and a few odds and ends. The top part she covered in floor to ceiling book shelves; each of them bursting at the seams with her favorite books.

Myriam settled herself in her chair, took a sip of her coffee, closing her eyes to really savor the moment.

***

Lily dropped her bags at the door. After nearly twenty-fours of travel she couldn't believe it... she arrived in paradise. Berry Bay Island the exact slice of Heaven she needed. The damp air around her smelled of night blooming Jasmine and mint. The French doors of her staff cottage opened onto the white sandy beach and rolling waves of the sea.

She peeled off her tank top and booty shorts. Naked, she strolled out to the deserted beach and plunged into the ocean. The water felt like sun-warmed silk caressing her limbs as she glided through the gentle waves. No longer feeling the grim of the airports on her, she turned on her back and the let waves carry her back to shore.

The breeze felt amazing against her skin. Like phantom hands everywhere on her, teasing her. When she walked out of the water her nipples were hard little pebbles. She raised her hands to cup them in an attempt to curb the unexplainable rush of desire that invaded her.

No matter how aroused she felt, weariness took over. She stumbled onto the soft king size bed and fell...

Joss and his friends Kalan, Luke, Marcus, Nate and Oliver watched the raven haired beauty from they're favorite perch atop the cliff. She mesmerized them with her womanly curves, bountiful breasts – so full and round – invitingly luscious, their peaked nipples truly made their mouths water. Above all else, her self-confidence made her ultra sexy. Their cocks throbbed with carnal need.

Each of them sucked-in harsh quick breaths when she fell onto the huge bed. Six pairs of eyes nearly jumped out of their sockets when they watched slim fingers skimming down a curvy waist and bury themselves into what they could only imagine to be a tight, wet pussy.

On silent agreement they went down the path, strolled across the beach and passed through the threshold of the French doors...

Beep. Beep. Beep.

Max put down the manuscript with some reluctance and pressed the intercom key on his phone.

"Yes, Janine," he said

"Mr. Abraham, Darla is here to see you," his assistant's cheerful voice announced.

"Okay, let her in."

Max closed the manuscript and put it back on top of the pile on his desk.

"Darla, I didn't expect you in today." He greeted the tall dark blonde walking in.

"Arthur wanted me to check in with you and those," she said as she nodded her head towards the piles of manuscripts littering his desk. "Anything good?" She asked with a huge smile.

She knew that for the last six months every new submission received from well known authors to new ones fresh off the block had involved Jolly Old Saint Nick and the Spirit of Christmas in some shape or form. Max arched his brow to emphasize his response "Oh, you know, OH, OH, OHs and Old Man Winter and Advent and the magic creatures that are Santa's elves."

Even as he said this, a passage from manuscript he just put down swarmed into his mind. It had nothing to do with Saint Nick, or December 25th, it didn't involve elves or the North Pole. Fiery passion, lust, maybe even love he found it refreshing and couldn't wait to return to it; which bode very well indeed for one Misty Valentine – a unknown name to him. Could it be that he would be the one to make this new author's dreams come true?

"In that case, I'll let you get back to it." The smile on her face reached her baby blue eyes which made them twinkle with delight and something more; an invitation.

Max couldn't deny that Darla's beauty. A very beautiful woman indeed; nearly six feet tall and nearly all of it legs, trim athletic legs, slim waist, flat stomach, perfect lemon breasts that would fit perfectly in the palms of his hands. Full pouty lips, high cheek bones, and those baby blues inviting him in. She made it clear that she did not have any issues mixing business with pleasure. It happened from time to time in the past that he too, mixed business with pleasure. So what stopped him now? Her smile didn't falter, but when he did not respond to her invitation the light dimmed in her eyes. Her voice fell just a bit less cheerful when she said

"Well, Ok then. Night Max."

"Night Darla, let Arthur know I'll send him my recommendations by early next week."

"Will do," she said and before she could click the door shut she added "don't burn the midnight oil again."

"I won't," he promised.

He settled himself comfortably in his chair, picked up Misty Valentine's manuscript *Enter Sandman* and flicked it open with his thumb.

His cock twitched.

"Now you decide to wake up," he groaned just as his cell phone chimed. He pulled out the vibrating device from his pocket. No wonder his cock sprang to life, it responded to her – invitation or not – anytime of the day or night.

She'd been the star of his very first wet dream. He remembered it well. They were twelve and had spent the entire day at the lake. They chased after frogs and dug up worms to bait their hooks. They fished until they ran out of bait and swam out to the island where some of the other boys started teasing her about her voluptuous chest. They told her that her swimsuit padding would sink to the bottom of the lake and then she'd be flat as a board like all the other girls. She'd gotten so mad that she'd pulled down her swimsuit and gave everyone an eyeful of her perfect full and firm pineapple breasts. That night he dreamt of touching those white ovals and he woke up the next morning on sticky sheets. Over the years he watched in amazement as the ovals of her breasts grew fuller and firmer until a luscious pair of Es, *how he'd been embarrassed when... no don't go there...* sat high on her chest. The fact that twenty years later she, and her magnificent breasts, still starred in many of his erotic dreams did not elude him.

One day, he silently promised his growing shaft, and pressed on the talk button.

"Hello, Myriam."

"Max." Her voice told him that he'd forgotten something. But what? "I am sorry," he said automatically.

"Hum, for what?" She asked.

He really didn't know. "You got me. I don't know. I know I need to apologize I obliviously forgot something. Please, tell me what?"

"Oh, Max." She laughed.

The rich vibrant sound coursed through him and ignited a fire low in his belly. His ever growing cock pulsed to the rhythm of her laughter.

"You were supposed to meet me silly, at the mall. Remember? Christmas shopping."

The mall.

Shopping.

He hated shopping. So did Myriam. By tradition they went together. That way it made the gruesome task less ominous.

"God, I am so *so* sorry Myriam. I'll leave now. Meet you in the ..."

"... No, Max. I've had enough of this place for one day. We'll do it another time. I am heading home."

"I'll bring you your favorite Thai soup as a peace offering," he suggested.

"Sounds good, see you soon," she said and clicked off.

Max took a minute to cool his raging hormones and get his cock to settle back down. The weight of the manuscript in his hands didn't help. For he knew the sexy story could bring images of his own carnal dreams to light. He flipped it closed and deftly put it in his battered leather satchel. He glanced at his desk, as he always did when picking up his old bag, and smiled at the burnt copper haired girl smiling back at him through the glass frame.

"Tell me what to do," he whispered at her.

His stomach growled, reminding him that he hadn't eaten anything since this morning, his cup of coffee and half toasted bagel were long gone leaving him famished. He closed the lights and headed out bringing with him a gust of cold air that had suddenly filled the room.

***

December 12 (later during the day)

Juls,

He'll be here soon. Now that I've made up my mind to snag him, sort-a-speak, I feel nervous. The butterflies are overwhelmingly busy.

What if I screw everything up?

103

What if he laughs in my face when I tell him I want him... that I love him?

What.

If.

Two very normal words. Common words. They hold no impact whatsoever when separate. Put them together... what a punch they throw. What if? What if? What if? Each of my unanswered what ifs are blows straight to my heart – blows that have kept me from revealing this truth for so many years.

I can't lose him Juls. (*I've already lost you.*)

There it is. My biggest 'what if,' that spreads fear and ice into my veins. What if I do this, reveal my true feelings for him, and he doesn't feel the same? Will I, *no*, can I still be is friend if he doesn't love me back? Will I end up losing him?

I can't do this. A moment of crazy hit me this morning that's all. I can't risk it. Or can I?

Ding Dong.

Did I just write that?

Ding Dong.

Yes I did.

The bell is ringing. My doorbell. He's here.

God, Juls. Tell me what to do.

The bell chimed in response to her last request. She threw her journal of pages on her bed and ran down the stairs in such a hurry that she did not notice the curtains of her closed window ruffle to and fro. She reached the last step with a bounce and pulled open the front door.

"Hi Max. Let me take those," she said as she reached for the bags of takeout food.

Her fingers brushed against his and the butterflies heated her belly. She knew they wouldn't let her hide her feelings for much longer. It's not the Holiday frenzies that urged her to put her crazy seduction plan into action. It's the damn butterflies. Without hesitation, she pulled him out of the cold December night and into a warm hug.

"Hey beautiful," he said into her hair. "I know what you're doing. And it won't work," he teased.

Her heat stopped. How could he know?

"You're only trying to get the food away from me so you can sneak one my shrimp rolls," he teased.

Her heart resumed beating.

"Guilty," she said as she reluctantly pulled out of the hug.

Max followed her in the kitchen. Set the bags on table, including his leather satchel. And then went to put away his jacket in the front hall closet. Myriam's eyes watered at the sight of the familiar bag. Her hand moved over it, the leather worn and soft under her touch brought the tears she could no longer hold back. She could still feel the embossed lettering they'd custom ordered at the bottom the overlapping front. The letters M. A. were still perfectly aligned with the closing buckles.

"You ready to eat," Max asked when he returned to the kitchen.

Myriam blinked her eyes quickly. She didn't want to explain her tears. "Yeah, I am starved," she turned around and pulled out two plates from the cupboard.

"So did you have a nice day," he asked around a mouth full of curry noodles.

"Yeah, you,"

"I guess,"

They both looked at each other and started laughing.

"What in the heck happened there?" He asked.

"I don't know."

She did know – the butterflies clogged her up. She needed to relax.

"Actually, my day sucked. I had to grade the short stories for my online Creative Writing class. I swear Max, these new students don't know what a dictionary or spell check is. When they do use these tools, the pieces are littered with crazy synonyms for simplest words. Out of 45 students only 22 submitted their assignments on time. So of course, I spent half the day listening to excuses for late assignment returns, or no assignments done. To top it all off, none of my students were creative. At all. Over and over again the same theme reoccurred. God! If I have to read another Seasonal expose, I'll pull my hair out."

He chuckled.

"I know what you mean," he groaned. "Darla came to see me this evening. Arthur is impatient. He wants my selection. Honestly, Myriam, I don't feel like publishing another Holiday novel. I want to end the year with something different."

The butterflies in her stomach went wild. *This is the time to propose something different. Isn't it? I can't* she told the swarm invading her and fought to keep them under tight control.

"You want dessert."

"Sure, you know I always have room for something sweet."

He said it so casually, but something different burned in his eyes or could it be that her over active butterflies were putting things in her mind that really weren't there at all? She searched his face to see any signs of what? Arousal? Love? She didn't know and dropped her gaze to the table.

"I made some apple fritters this afternoon."

"What are you waiting for woman, bring one over."

Myriam bustled around the kitchen brewing coffee, serving the sweet dish onto plates, pulling out cream from fridge and honey from the top shelf of the cupboard. All the while she felt his eyes on her – caressing her limbs as she bent and stretched. Or maybe the butterflies were in fact screwing her senses. Nonetheless, her cheeks warmed and flushed rosy pink. Her heart raced in her chest. She took in a deep breath to steady her hands before she pulled down their favorite mugs and brought everything to the table.

"Here let me," he said and poured the hot rich liquid into their mugs he added a few drops of cream in each and a dollop of honey in his. Something flared in his eyes when they locked on hers as his mouth closed over a forkful of apple delight. This time, she knew the butterflies didn't make her see that flare of what? Desire? Hunger? What? It had been too quick and short lived for her to decipher.

"Christ, that's good," he exhaled.

That explained it, hunger and desire, but not for her, only to soothe a craving sweet tooth. She sipped her coffee and left her apple fritter untouched on her plate. Pleasure infused her as she watched him. His burnt cooper hair all tousled, hazel eyes closed in a moment of savor as he took the last bite off his plate. Chiseled features soften by the dessert invoked bliss etched into them. Full luscious lips nibbling and licking.

Christ, the butterflies were off again; racing as fast as her pulse. *Breathe. Breathe.* She reminded her lungs.

"You gonna eat that?"

Myriam couldn't control the sensual giggle that bubbled out of her. "Here," she said and pushed her untouched sweet to him. Again, she enjoyed watching him close his eyes and savor every bite. She knew he would be off soon. If she wanted to seduce him tonight, she needed to get a move on. She remained at a lost as to what to say, what to do. It's not every day you tell someone you've known for thirty years that you want him to ravish you forever because you're in love with him. Her English Lit and Creative Writing masters didn't come to her rescue. She found no words to express the feelings that had been building inside of her since the tender age of thirteen for this man – her best friend.

"Myriam?"

Oh, he obviously said or asked something that she missed.

"Huh, sorry, what?"

"You okay, you looked so far away there for a minute."

"Yes, I am OK. It's mesmerizing sometime watching you eat." The words flew out of her mouth before she could stop them.

"Mesmerizing. Really? Please I am all ears."

Could this be it? The moment... To tell him ...

＊

All night Max sensed something different about her.

From the moment she hugged him hello. His mind went into wishful thinking mode or had it? It sure felt like she pressed her body more tightly to his than usual. He didn't complain of course, the feel of her in his arms even through his bulky leather jacket had stirred his senses. The smell of her hair intoxicated him far more then the sweet dessert he'd just finished. And now with all his senses raw from wanting her so much, she dropped this bomb shell on him. He sent a silent plea to the Heavens and patiently waited for her response.

"Max, honestly, how can I not be mesmerized by a grown man being reduced to the glee of a five year old in a sweet shop with every bite he takes of his dessert," she teased.

Thanks a lot he grumbled to the Heavens *you were no help at all.*

"It's only 'cause you made them and they were so lusciously sweet and tart – the perfect bite every time. I couldn't help but to fully appreciate the treat," he replied with more seriousness then the situation warranted. He willed himself to relax. It's not her fault she didn't give him the answer he wanted to hear. Wishful thinking after all; his acute yearning for her made him feel so out of sorts. He didn't dare hope, yet, she'd seemed so responsive to his gaze. Her skin looked so lovely all rosy pink. He wanted to believe that *he* did that to her. Usually, at this point that he would put a lid on his desire for her, he just didn't want to anymore.

He wanted to drag her to him. Crush his mouth on those pouty pink lips and tangle his tongue with hers in a timeless dance of passion. He wanted to feel the silkiness of her creamy skin underneath his palm, his body. His cock rose at the lustful thoughts of her naked: auburn hair fanned out on his pillow case, lips swollen from kisses, breasts heaving with each of her shallow breathes, nipples hard and extended, thighs quivering with need, dripping wet pussy waiting to be filled. Christ, he nearly came in his shorts at the thought of being buried deep inside her soft velvety walls. To imagine the feel of them tightening against his raging hard-on nearly undid him. He wanted nothing more than her – heart, body, soul – he wanted it all.

Now if only he could find the words to tell her. How much she meant to him. How much he wanted her in his life forever and not only as his best friend, but as a lover – a wife. A grin spread over his face as an image of her belly swollen with child – his child – filtered through his mind.

"What's that smile for," she asked

Dare he tell her?

"Nothing," he chickened out.

"So, what have you brought this time," she asked eyeing the satchel that had been left at the other end of the table.

He hadn't realized that he'd brought in with him. Normally, he only brought in his work bag when he wanted her opinion on a manuscript he felt on the fence about. He didn't feel on the fence about the one burning a hole in his satchel at the present time. He knew he would recommend to Arthur a publishing contract with full advance to the author.

"A manuscript I need to finish reading before writing up my recommendations. It's the only one I've received that's actually *not* obsessed with Christmas."

"How refreshing, can you share?"

"Not right now. I think this one will go to print."

"Wow. So you've found your something different."

There's so much he wanted to tell her. Like how he wished things between them could be different. "In a book, yes," he replied hoping she'd want more out of that statement. She didn't disappoint him.

"What does that mean?"

Now that the door opened for him he didn't know how to cross it. His mouth opened. No words formed on his lips. He closed it, swallowed hard and tried again. Still no words felt right to explain the depth of his feelings for her. I love you seemed to fall short. They'd shared those words before – a life time ago under a rain-soaked umbrella – they'd looked at each other and mouthed those words. He didn't want to think about that day. He shook his head to dislodge the gray scene from there.

"Max," her soft voice filled with concern brought him out of his nightmare.

"Nothing."

"Huh?"

"Sorry, what did you say?"

"Nothing. Just waiting for you to explain your..."

"...Oh, I only meant that I am sure this manuscript is the ticket to end the year with a bang."

"Oh."

Something flashed in her gray-blue eyes. Disappointment? Longing? He couldn't tell. Even though her eyes were always talking, like the sky, they could be as gray as the storm clouds moving in or so clear a blue just like a clean horizon after the squall. Right now, they were that in between color. Not gray. Not blue. Just the perfect mix of both that could easily conceal any of her emotions.

He wished. Damn enough of this. He reached out and pushed away a strand of her heavy auburn tresses. His fingers burned to wrap themselves around the silken strands; to pull her face close to him, take her. Brand her as his. Instead, he let go of her hair and whispered. "I should go."

She didn't stop him. Tell him to stay and spend the night. She simply guided him to the front hall. Opened the closet doors reached in and pulled out his jacket. He shrugged it on and she eased herself into his arms – hugging him. Her body pressed against his to the point that he felt her wonderful breasts flattened against his padded chest.

"Night," she whispered as she pulled away from him.

As much as he wanted to, he didn't dare to drag her back to him. He knew that if this started, he wouldn't be able to stop himself. He needed to be sure of her feelings for him before...

"Night," he said and softly clicked the door shut.

He took in long gulps of the frigid night air and leaned his head back against the door. In the wind he could have sworn that he heard a soft bell-like voice chiding him *"You fool. You missed it. The moment you've been waiting for. She wanted you to kiss her."*

He wanted to glare at the unseen voice but the hairs at his nape rose. Goosebumps covered his flesh. *You win* he silently said and pulled his jacket tighter against him and went to his car.

***

Myriam sighed and leaned against the closed door.

The front hall felt cold without him near her. Words danced across the chilliness and penetrated her mind.

"Myr, you should have made your move. When you plastered yourself to him with that hug you should have tilted your head upwards and you would have found his lips ready and hungry. Stop being afraid of all your pesky what ifs. They're unfounded. Trust me."

Myriam shivered from head to toe as an icy shiver ran up and down her spine. After a few moments of trembling uncontrollably heat slowly returned to her limbs. She closed the lights and headed upstairs. The grandfather clock chimed the first ring of midnight.

December 13

The clock just changed Juls. Christmas is now a day closer. And I think I missed it... my chance.

I want to trust you, Juls.

I do. *Really*. But I am scared.

I need to know he loves me before I can let anything happen.

111

Myriam eyelids drooped. Her journal slipped from her hands and she drifted off into sleep.

The morning dawned bright and cold.

Myriam picked-up her journal from the floor and put it away. She had a class to prepare for. All through the morning she kept her mind busy moving from one class video to the next. She posted the series online for her students. She checked her email accounts. One of them remained dormant; a secret one... that no one knew anything about. Not even her best friend. *Especially,* not her best friend! *Oh well.* She sighed. No news is good news. The other overflowed with requests from her students. She replied to each one. By two in the afternoon she shut down her computer and climbed up the polished staircase. She picked one of her old favorites and sank into a buttery leather chair.

She woke in a start, in a pitch-dark room. When had she fallen asleep? What time is it? She didn't wear a watch and the darkness made it impossible to check out the pendulum clock on the wall. She stretched her stiff muscles and rose. Myriam climbed down the stairs and picked-up her cell phone from her desk. 9:36 pm. 3 missed calls, 4 text messages. She unlocked her phone and scroll through the text messages first:

Miss Volterre, I swear I meant to send my piece... she deleted the message. She'd deal with Jeremiah later

Myriam want to reschedule our shopping expedition. I am free this evening.

Myriam?

Guess you're busy. I'm flying to TO in the morning for a string of meetings. I'll be back in time. Call if you need anything.

Next she checked her voice mail:

Miss Volterre I sent you a text, but I felt it important for me... she saved Jeremiah's message for later

Hang up – deleted

Myriam, Max's voice sounded breathless as he sighed her name, I'll be in Toronto for only a couple of days. I'll be there I swear.

Tears ran down her cheeks as he told her bye and clicked off his message.

Oh great good God.

Max would be out of reach for days.

Without thinking she rushed down the stairs and flew out of the house.

***

Max hadn't been able to get her out of his head since he'd left her place last night. The smell of her – coconut, vanilla – fresh and sweet intoxicated him. His palm grew moist when he texted her to reschedule their shopping date. When he didn't get a reply his heart plummeted to the pit of his stomach. He tried calling her and hung up on her voice mail.

Shit!

He couldn't leave for days – especially not this close to, no he didn't want to think about that – and not say good-bye. He'd called back and left a message that barely made sense and threw himself in his work.

Joss and his friends peeled off their boardies and let them fall in pools around the king size bed.

Nate nodded to Joss. As if on cue all the other guys nodded as well. Pleased that they were all in agreement, after all, women boasted that they could come only to the sound of his voice, Joss cleared his throat and began humming an Aussie lullaby and brushed his hand over the slim fingers moving between the half-open thighs.

"Sleep angel, sleep. Let us adore you," he hushed as he moved his fingers with hers.

His thumb found her pulsing clit and circled it.

She moaned.

"That's right angel, open your mouth," he coaxed and applied more pressure on her clit.

She moaned deeper. Fully parting her lips and Kalan slip his engorged cock inside. In a pure animalistic response she sucked him deep. His eyes closed. Fuck, he nearly lost it! Her mouth so hot, so incredible had him pulsing like a teenager receiving is very first blow job.

Joss worked her fingers free of her tight wet pussy and guided them to Luke's curved dick. Ladies had raved and raved about that infamous curve of his. He hadn't fully believed it until he watched this slumbering Goddess sigh in pleasure, around a mouth full of cock, as her fingers wrapped around the curve appreciatively.

The unexpected sharp thud of knuckles on the solid oak frame of his front door pulled Max out of the alluring scene that one Misty Valentine brought to light and let the manuscript fall to the floor. The echoing sound of the knuckles beating on his door almost felt alive; like a beating heart calling to him. He hurried towards his front door and pulled it open.

Like a whirlwind Myriam threw her arms around his neck and pulled his head down. Her lips hovered over his. Their hot breaths mixed together before she softly pressed her trembling lips to his and whispered "Come. Back."

Max's mind didn't register Myriam's disheveled appearance. Actually, his mind didn't register anything at all. He felt. Felt her: in his arms, her warm breath tickling – torturing – him. Felt her lips on his. The moment her soft delicious lips touched his, a fire spread inside of him. A scorching heat burned him through and through. Before he could realize what happened she vanished. There he stood on the stoop of his front porch. Dazzled and confused. He lifted his head in time to see Myriam's tail light turn the corner.

Not a dream.

Max closed his door.

What. The. Hell? He wondered.

His cock pushed against his zipper. He crossed the foyer and walked into the guest bathroom. He turned the water on cold and stepped into the shower. Eyes closed he lifted his head to let the frigid beads rain down on him. Even with the cold water battering him, his cock still throbbed. He wrapped his fingers around his erection. God, her lips felt incredible. He stroked from base to tip. So soft. Then stroked from tip to base. So delicious. The rhythm increased. She kissed me. His hand went wild. On my lips. It moved like a blur over the tight skin of his cock.

Max wanted more of that sweet mouth of hers. His balls hardened. He imagined it on his jaw. His grip tightened around his girth. He pictured it closing over his nipples. His butt cheeks squeezed together. He envisioned those luscious lips wrapped around his cock. Hot come spurted out of him in long gushes. He dropped his gaze to the stall floor and watched the white ribbons of his pent up desire swirled down the drain.

***

December 13 (late evening)

Holly. Christ. Juls, I – I – I kissed him.

For only a brief instant I pressed my mouth to his. My heart nearly stopped in my chest. The butterflies swirled and twirled low in my belly. My blood boiled in my veins. WANTING MORE.

I ran.

I left him there starting after my tail lights.

He's going to Toronto. I couldn't just let him leave. Did I do the right thing Juls?

Wish you were here.

Miss you like crazy.

xoxox

Myriam closed her journal and put it under her pillow.

Her Friday student workshops were a hit and the rest of the weekend went by in blur. On Monday morning Myriam booted up her laptop and opened up her emails – *the secret one still remained dormant*. She sighed and went about with her work. Constantly distracted by the butterflies as they fluttered nervously in the pit of her stomach, she stopped writing and glanced at the clock.

Out of time if she didn't want to be late, she saved her work, took another quick look at her emails – *still nothing* – and shut down her laptop.

Dressed in her favorite cowl neck top and pencil skirt she bounded down the stairs and pulled out her soft knee-high leather boots from the closet. She pulled them on one at a time and checked her reflection in the mirror. Her cheeks were rosy pink. Her eyes shimmered like dark blue-gray clouds. Her hair, well her auburn tresses were always a handful to subdue, so they tumbled down her shoulders in various waves and ringlets. Her breasts swelled above the scoop of her cowl neckline. Her curvy waist and curvier hips hugged the seams of her sweater. The pencil skirt slimmed down her thighs and rested above her bare knees. The boots were like second skin on her calves. She applied a small amount of Wildberry lip gloss, grabbed her jacket and scarf and left the house.

She drove down the familiar Ottawa streets, zipping through the main fares without much traffic and urned onto the long entrance and slowed down her speed.

The deserted parking sunk her spirits.

He'll be here. He promised.

She parked at the end of lot, got out and strolled down the path towards...

***

Max watched her from a distance. She looked beautiful with her head bowed on her chin and tears freely running down her wind-kissed cheeks. He silently made his way to her.

"Thought I'd find you here," he whispered.

"I miss her Max. Miss her like crazy."

Max tore his gaze away from her and finally settled them on the tombstone:

In loving Memory of Julianna Abraham
Beloved daughter, sister and friend.
We miss you angel.
Born 10-26-1981 Died 12-17-2002

"I miss her too," he murmured.

They held each other in comfortable silence. The air around them picked up. Cold wind sent shivers down his spine. Myriam trembled in his arms. He tightened his hold on her. She leaned into him. His heart swelled. So did his cock.

"Sorry sis," he sent to her in the Heavens. The sun broke through the cover of clouds in response. He knew his twin understood and smiled up at the soft ray of light.

"You want to go?"

"Not yet," her reply came out muffled by the bulkiness of his jacket.

He reached down, traced her cheek. Took her chin between his fingers and tilted her head upwards. He stared into her eyes; giving her a chance to stop him.

She didn't.

He bent his head down slowly; still giving her a chance to pull away.

She didn't.

He softly brushed his lips to hers.

"Do you know how crazy I've been since you did that to me," he whispered but didn't wait for her to reply. He tilted her head an inch more and traced her bottom lip with his tongue. Her soft throaty moan nearly undid him. He parted her lips further and slipped his tongue inside her mouth. She tasted of fresh air and snow and sun and tears – so very, very sweet.

He stroked her tongue with his and nibble on its tip with his teeth. Her fingers dug into his hair – holding him closer to her. Her tongue twirled around his. His lungs burned. His heart raced. He felt weak in the knees. Light headed. Desire burst through his every pore. He couldn't take her here. He needed to break away from this soul-searing kiss and get her in bed.

Now!

He held her face in the palms of his hands and slowed down the kiss. Reluctantly he lifted his lips away and moved his eyes on hers to search them. They were clear blue. Pure happiness shone through them. He knew that his eyes mirrored the same thing back at her.

"I am taking you home."

He leaned down and kissed her again. He couldn't get enough of her.

"We're going. Now," he growled.

They walked back to the parking lot hand in hand. They reached their cars. He didn't want to separate from her. She leaned into him and kissed him.

"See you at my place," she whispered and got into her car.

Max followed her out and down the avenues. The traffic seemed to be in his favor and remained light. The lights stayed green. They reached her place in less than twenty minutes. He parked and reached her as she twisted the knob open. They rushed into the hall. His hands were in her hair. Her throat arched back. His lips crushed down on hers – devouring – he'd fasted for too long. He couldn't curb his passion any longer. Her hands were everywhere in his hair, on his shoulders, on his chest, *Oh God,* low on his chest. He released her lips and grabbed her wrists. He couldn't take her here in the vestibule. He pulled her along and climbed up the stairs. They reached her bedroom door stumbled through it and fell on her bed.

Max cupped her face in his hands and kissed her gently. Locked his eyes on hers and watch them grow dark when he whispered "I love you, Myriam."

"I love you, too."

She kissed him long and passionately. Ran her hands down his chest till her fingers grabbed the hem of his shirt and pulled it up. She molded herself to his naked torso traced her fingers over his abs and belly button. Her nails scratch up. Her palms lay flat on his pectorals. His breath hitched. Hot. His skin felt on fire everywhere she touched. He crushed his mouth on hers when her fingers circled and pinched his nipples. Hard, rock-hard, his cock painfully pushed against his slacks. He warped his hands around her head. Tugged it back upwards, exposing the long column of her throat. His mouth moved down and licked the wildly pulsing vein behind her earlobe. He sucked on it.

Her hands left his nipples and travelled south. Way down south. Her fingers plunged and unbuttoned his fly. Frozen in bliss he stayed still. His breathe came in and out in short ragged pulls. Myriam pushed down his pants and briefs. His cock sprang free and stood at rigid attention. Tentatively she ran her nails down the length of him. Fireworks exploded in his mind. He lost all thoughts. Like an animal he ravaged her neck, tore open her sweater. Ripped up her bra and bit down on her rosy beaded nipple. His hand squeezed her other breast tight – tighter – he knew she'd have marks in the morning. Yet, he couldn't stop possessing her.

Myriam's fingers were firmly clasped around his erection. Moving up and down the length of it. Her fingers applied more pressure at the base and twirled around the head. Small nails scratched his blood infused purple head. Drawing beads of pre-cum. She dipped her finger in his small hole. Milking more cum from him. With her eyes locked on his she raised her finger and sucked it into her mouth. Max pushed her down on the bed. His hands cupping, caressing, teasing, her naked, curvy torso until they reached down to her skirt, he pushed it down and looked in amazement at the moist, engine red lace triangle covering her up. The alluring under garment made his blood boil. His lips touched, nipped and kissed everywhere his hands had been. They hovered over that tantalizing red lace. He took in long arousing breaths. She smelled divine – musky and rich – pure woman. He pushed up on his arms and looked for her eyes.

They stormed. Dark gray. Darker blue.

Max skimmed the hem of her panties with his fingers. Her breasts move up and down. Faster and faster with each of her panting breaths. Even though he didn't think it could be possible, her eyes grew darker still. He reached her round hips and gently pulled on the strings. He slid her underwear down to her ankles and let them fall to the floor. His gaze hungrily possessed every inch of her. His nostrils flared. The smell of her arousal intoxicated his senses.

"Myriam, you're so beautiful."

She blushed. Not just her cheeks. Her entire body flushed a rosy pink. Sexy. So incredibly sexy. He kissed her ankle and worked a series of hot wet kiss the length of her inner leg. Her nails dug in his back as he neared her exposed glistening pussy. Unable to resist the tasty treat any longer he plunged his tongue inside. Christ she felt tight – so tight – he'd never felt anything like this before. Her nails scrapped his scalp as she pulled on his tousled burnt copper crop and pushed his face closer to her slit. His nose bumped her sensitive clit. He wiggled it over the hard numb. His tongue darted in and out of her molten core. Her hips thrashed on his face. Max licked her slit, his tongue setting a quick up and down rhythm. Up. Down. Up. Down. It moved faster and faster. Her pelvis arched.

Max latched her clit between his lips. His hands trailed up her torso to fondle, squeeze and pinch her breasts and rock hard nipples. Hot. Her skin felt so hot underneath his touch. He released her clit and moved his mouth upwards. Licking her hour glass curves. Nibbling her belly button. Caressing her abs. Worshiping her breasts in the way he'd always dreamt about. They were soft and heavy and perfect. He'd never get enough of those luscious ovals. Her hands and nails were creating intricate design on his skin as they trailed down to wrap themselves around his erection.

He couldn't breathe. It felt that good when she touched him. He watched in stunned silence as she moved down the bed, laid flat on her stomach, opened her mouth and took him in. His hands lovingly held her head. Her mouth inched down lower, lower until her nose flattened on his abdomen. He wanted to pump so badly, but remained still as her throat muscles relaxed and swallowed him deeper. His fingers curled tighter in her tresses. His balls squeezed against his ass.

Fire. Everywhere. Skin too hot. Senses to too raw. Her mouth sucking. Her teeth nibbling. Her tongue stroking the veins pulsing erratically under the tight skin of his cock. He released her hair and ran his hand down her back. He fondled her ass. Squeezed her butt cheeks. Ran his finger along her crack. Found the entrance to her dripping wet pussy. He slipped a finger inside. Tight, so damn tight. Her tongue played with his cock slit. She plunged the tip of it inside. He moved his finger inside her velvety walls. She bobbed down on his cock, squeezed his ball sack in her palms.

Sanity left him.

Max slipped his finger out of her. Pull out of her mouth. Flipped her around. Savagely crushed his mouth to hers. Bit her bottom lip and moved down to suck on that bulging vein under her earlobe. With his lips against her hammering pulse he thrust into her with animalistic force. The resistance he felt and the shudder of pain that stiffened her body cut through him.

Sanity returned.

He wanted to pull out. Go slow. Her legs wrapped around his waist in a vice grip. Her hips undulated – grounded, gyrated – she squeezed his cock so tight. Her wet heat coated him as he stretched her to the limit. Again and again she squeezed his cock into her enveloping heat. It spread through him and made his blood boil. His lungs burned. His heart raced. He plunged deeper inside, seeking more of that addictive heat, and set a cruel rhythm as he pushed and pulled in out of her incredibly tight pussy. Her hips meet each of his violent thrusts. Her breasts bobbed wildly. Her pulse danced under his lips. Her teeth sank into his shoulder as he pounded harder and faster into her.

Sweat-slicked her skin flushed a deeper red. Sexy – so fucking sexy. His balls tightened – hardened – squeezed against his ass. Almost there. Christ, he needed to bring her there. He plunged in so deep he hit her cervix. She clawed his back. His mouth unlatched from her throbbing pulse and licked down to her pebbled nipple. He circled it and sucked it in to the warm confines of his greedy mouth. His cock moved faster and faster. His mouth sucked her nipple harder and deeper. His fingers reached down between them and found her clit. He rolled it around and flicked it over and over again. He never stopped thrusting in and out her extremely tight delicious pussy.

"Max," she cried out "don't stop. Please don't stop."

Her words propelled him onwards. Like a maniac he plunged in and out of her wet tight folds. He bit down on her nipple. Her body trembled. Her breath came in guttural rasps. He grunted deep in his throat. He claimed her lips in another soul searing kiss. Her hot cream flowed over the tight sensitive skin of his cock mixing with his gushing sperm. Her pussy overflowed. Warm sticky juices oozed down her thighs and covered his. He trembled all over. His hand shook as they gently cupped her face. He broke off their kiss and searched her eyes for any signs of regret or pain. He'd been insane taking her like that. Once he'd realized that she'd been untouched he should have been tender. Not a wild beast. Her eyes closed. Long lashes caressed her creamy skin. She stretched under him like a satisfied cat. He touched his nose to hers.

"Open your eyes Myriam."

Her eyes locked on his.

"Why didn't you say anything? I – I -"

"You what? Would have stopped?" Even with a note of defiance in it, her voice sounded close to tears.

"No, I couldn't have stopped. I have wanted you for too long for that. But Myriam, I would have used every ounce of gentleness to worship your body."

"Oh, I don't know what to say," she whispered.

"Are you okay? Did I hurt you?"

Max needed to know that he didn't hurt by his savage lovemaking. A soft smile curled her lips.

"Well, seeing as this my first time, I don't know. Is it normal for my body to feel deliciously enervated or for my skin to hum everywhere you touched it with your hands, your lips, your tongue?"

He grew hard inside her as her soft words spread joy and fire everywhere inside of him.

"God yes, Myriam, it's normal. Feel." He took her hand and pressed it on his damp skin.

"You're so hot and your heart is racing. Like mine," she said and brought his palm over her left breast.

"I love you."

"I love you."

***

The butterflies in Myriam's belly swarmed and twirled spreading a fire everywhere inside of her.

He loved her.

He wanted to worship her body.

She'd been so scared that he wouldn't have wanted her due to her lack of experience. It's not every day a man comes across a thirty-two year old virgin. She'd known long ago, that her virginity belonged to Max. All of her belonged to Max. She bent down her head and claimed his lips for a kiss.

His cock hardened and expanded inside of her stretching her sensitive inner walls. The sensation as his cockhead pushed against her cervix sent her pulse racing. She squeezed him – hard and slow. He moved slowly and pushed her down on the mattress. In a gentle manner he slipped in and out. His mouth so soft on her skin left a trail of fiery need. Need which pulsed straight to her clit. His fingers skimmed over her humming skin in a sweet caress.

This slow torture had her nerve endings sparking out shards of hot desire everywhere inside her. She closed her eyes and relished each new sensation: a kiss here, a touch there, a pull, a push, another kiss, another touch, more pushing in, more pulling out. His mouth and hands covered every inch of her over sensitized skin. His cock, so hard, so thick, stroked against her clit in a languid fashion. Then it would enter her one inch at a time. And pull out just as slowly. Her lungs filled with liquid fire. The butterflies swarmed and twirled crazily. Her pulse hammered.

"More Max," she begged.

He chuckled against her breast and blew his warm breath on her wet nipple. Shivers danced down her spine. She arched her back. Tilted her pelvis taking in him deeper – so deep – yet not deep enough. His mouth closed over her extended nipple. His tongue circled it, flicked it, then he sucked and sucked and sucked some more. When he released it she heard a little pop. He gave her other nipple the same delicious treatment. Heat radiated from his pores as she caressed his bare back. She loved to feel his muscle constrict and relax as he moved in and out of her.

She kissed his neck. Tasted his salty musky sweat. Yum, addictive. She licked and kissed his throat. His grip on her hips tightened. His breath became ragged. His muscles contracted under her wandering hands. She suckled and nibbled his neck and shoulders. His cock moved in bold quick thrusts. She repeatedly squeezed his cockhead as he tried to pull it out. He grunted and claimed her lips. He plunged inside of her. She screamed in ecstasy. As if propelled by her screams and moans he plunged deeper, faster and harder. The deeper and faster and harder he moved the more she wanted. Her body thrashed under his – her pelvis arching up to meet each of his wild plunges. Her back lifted up the bed as he plunged in and out of the velvet embrace like a demon on fire. Her pussy flooded. Their juices mixed and swirled down her thighs again.

"God, you're amazing," she whispered in his mouth.

"No. You're amazing," he whispered back.

In slow motion he pulled out of her hot, wet, tight folds and rolled on his back and straight out of bed. He lifted her in his arms. She wrapped her arms around his neck and he marched them both in her en-suite bath. Cradling her to his chest, he turned on the taps and began to fill the claw-footed tub. He gently laid her down in the rising hot water. Myriam relaxed in the warmth and closed her eyes. Sometime later, she felt him slip in behind her. Her eyes fluttered open.

"Where'd you go?"

"I changed the sheets on the bed."

Embarrassed heat flushed her cheeks.

"Why you blushing," he asked in a soft tone.

"I-I don't know. Guess I feel like I should have cleaned-up *that mess.*" Her cheeks redden some more.

He kissed her pink nose.

"Why do think that."

"Cause of the blood and the ..." she couldn't get the words out.

He kissed her lips.

"Myriam, I am the luckiest man alive." He swallowed hard and it seemed to her that he searched for his words "Never in my wildest dream could have dared hope that you..." He stopped as if uncomfortable to finish is train of thought so he changed course "I mean that I would be your first. Please don't ever be embarrassed to have shared that with me," he pleaded.

"Yes," Myriam said.

"Yes, what?"

"Yes, I saved myself for you," she answered the question he hadn't dared to ask.

He took her into his arms and gave a long tender kiss. They broke apart panting.

"Let me wash your hair."

She dunked her head under the water and handed him the bottle of coconut vanilla shampoo. His hands lovingly gathered her long tresses and lathered them up with the intoxicating sent. His fingers massaged her scalp as he worked in the shampoo. He rinsed her hair thoroughly and repeated the process with the conditioner.

"Ready to get out."

"Yes."

He lifted her out of the tub. Towel dried her body and wrapped the white soft terry-cloth towel around her mass of hair. He grabbed another towel and padded himself dry. She loved being cradled in his arms. The smell of his clean wet skin made her mouth water. She pressed her lips to his chest. She felt him shiver. She loved that she could do that to him. He laid her down on the freshly donned sheets and climbed in beside her. She rested her head on his chest. He kissed her earlobe and whispered "Sleep angel, sleep." The words were so familiar to her.

Could it be? A smile hovered on her lips as sleep claimed her.

***

In the stillness of the room Max watched the curtains of the closed window move to and fro. A smile touched his lips.

"Night sis," he said to the air and fell into slumber.

He woke up the next morning. Alone. He got up. Pulled on his pants and followed the rich Peruvian aroma.

"Morning beautiful," he said as he wrapped his arms around her.

"Morning."

She poured the coffee and handed him a brimming cup. He released her and took a sip.

"Delicious."

She pulled out plates and put half a toasted bagel on each. They ate. They kissed. They touched.

"I have to go. Arthur's expecting me at eleven."

She kissed him again – throwing her entire body into the kiss – her hips rolling over his cock, her hands everywhere on his body. He pushed her against the counter top lifted her ass onto the cold tiles. He fumbled to get his zipper down. She nipped his ear. Finally his zipper slid open. He drove his freed cock into her wet heat. Her lips fastened to his collar bone. Her tongue traced the length of it and moved upwards to his earlobe. He pulled out and drove back in. Her knees locked underneath his butt cheeks. She pressed him closer – deeper inside. His mouth found her nipple and captured it. She panted and clawed at his back. He pushed and pushed against her tight inner walls. She threw back her head on a long ragged moan. His balls smacked against her butt as he slammed harder and faster.

Her tightness drove him over the edge. He released the puffy nipple and captured the other one. Her fingers held his head in place. Her knees drew him nearer still, *and by God*, deeper inside that honeyed tightness. Hard and fast he plunged in and out of her molten core – long, hard, deep, fast – thrusts. One after the other – longer, harder, deeper, faster – so fast his legs shook from the effort. Her body bucked. He felt her hammering pulse against his chest. Yet, she followed his breakneck tempo as he pounded and pummeled and pulverized her pussy. His balls ached they were so hard and tight. Her hand reached down between them and pumped the base of his cock as he pulled in and out of her. Fireworks exploded behind his eyes. He filled her pussy with his thick come as her cream coated him. His legs still shook. Her body slumped over his in total bliss. He kissed her forehead and pulled out of her wet heat.

"You drive me crazy!" He cupped her face and kissed her.

She must have seen his reluctance to leave in his eyes because she gently pushed him away.

"You have to go. Arthur."

"I know."

Max tucked his now flaccid member in his briefs, pulled up his pants, picked up his jacket and left.

***

As soon as the door closed behind him Myriam ran up the stairs and threw herself on her bed. She pulled out her journal.

December 18.

OH. MY. GOD. Juls

We made love.

I am so happy I waited. I couldn't imagine wanting anyone else like I wanted him. I knew we belonged together. I swear our bodies were made for one another. Like two puzzle pieces locking together.

WOW.

He's a great lover. Sorry you probably didn't want to hear that about your twin brother. But I think I found perfection in him just the right mix of gentleman *and* wild beast at the same time.

Yes, I felt the pain of losing my virginity; in a flash he made forget it. Can you believe that he waited for me and we rode that wave of bliss together... is it always like this? I am so ready to find out.

I feel drained and sated and energized and I swear my body is humming.

Juls, I wish you were here to tell me that it's ok
for me to have Max like this. I think you would be
happy for us. I wish I knew for sure.

Miss you like crazy
xoxox

Myriam closed her journal with a sigh.

It'd been eleven years yesterday that one half of her best
friend died.

They were twenty one and Julianna had left the flat they shared
in the downtown core to go shopping. Myriam had fallen
asleep on the lumpy couch. The sound of the shrilling phone
woke her; she opened her eyes to a pit-dark flat and picked up
the annoying phone.

"Hello," she growled.

"Mrs. Abraham," a deep voice said

"No."

"May I speak with Mrs. Abraham please," the booming
voice requested

"She doesn't live here. Can I help you?"

A loud cough at other end of the line indicated that the
speaker cleared his throat before responding "I really need to
speak with Mr. or Mrs. Abraham."

"Well, they're in Europe. Let me get my roommate she's
their daughter," Myriam rested the phone in the crook of her
neck and called out for Julianna. When she didn't answer she
called again; louder, still no answer. Cold dread filled her.

She picked up the phone and barked "Who are you and
where is Julianna!"

Resigned the voice softened. "My name is Sergeant Storey."

Blood drained from her face. Her lungs failed. She couldn't
sure if he'd heard her when she said "Oh dear God,"

"What's your name miss,"

"Myriam Volterre. Julianna is my roommate and best friend. What happened?"

"There's been an accident. I'm afraid we couldn't save her."

The phone dropped from her icy fingers as she sank to the floor. The scream that tore out of her went on and on and on and on until Max wrapped his arms around her and rocked her against his frame. He rocked her until she fell asleep in his arms. Later he woke her and they called his parents.

They shared each other's grief that night and many nights after that. The morning of Julianna's funeral turned out to be gray and icy cold with rain pouring down from the Heavens. The heels of Myriam's boots sunk into the half frozen earth near the open grave. Max held an umbrella above their heads. They looked at each other and mouthed at the same time *I Love You.* The words had been expressed as a means of comfort then; last night when they shared those words again she knew the sentiment behind them rang true and pure.

With smile on her lips Myriam took a long hot shower. Her skin tingled when she wrapped herself in her bathrobe. She put on a pair of yoga pants and v-neck t-shirt. Bare feet she went downstairs and made her way to the back of the house pushed open the tower door and walked in. She booted up her laptop and padded back in the kitchen. She made fresh coffee and poured herself a cup. When she returned to her chair she glanced at the clock – already noon – logged in and check her emails. Coffee spurted out her mouth and nose.

Holly Mother of God.

She got mail. In her secret account!

Her fingers nervously clicked the message open. She read it. Re-read it. And read it again. She pinched her arm to make sure she hadn't walked into a dream. "Ouch!" She screamed. Okay not a dream. Even through the polite tone of the email she could tell he'd been excited when he wrote it. Her heart raced in her chest as she started to read out loud.

Dear Miss Valentine,

I am happy to announce that your manuscript *Enter Sandman* has been selected for publication.

Please find enclosed the publishing contract, offering you a full advance, as well as a few suggested changes to the piece, and cover art for your approval.

Return the signed contract and edited manuscript along with your art selection to me by no later than Friday, December 21, 2013, as we wish to launch your book by early February 2014.

I wish to express to you, Miss Valentine, my sincerest congratulations.

I look forward to meeting you soon.

Cordially,
Max Abraham
Senior Acquisition Agent & Editor
Arthur Blooms Publishing House

Myriam clasped a hand over her racing heart. Happiness filled her and quickly drained away. Cold dread moved in. Max replied. Max couldn't know. How would she tell him... her secret identity as Misty Valentine! Her cell phone skidded on her desk. She picked up the vibrating device and unlocked the screen.

A text.

Max: Thinking of u

Her hammering pulse danced faster and faster. Her fingers hovered over the key pad. I have to tell him. Not like this.

Me: Thinking of u 2

Seconds past and her phone buzzed again.

Max: I'll be at your place around 5.

Me: K

Max: Can't wait to see u

Me: Dido

Max: LOL

Me: ;)

Max: laters

Me: laters

The butterflies grew nervous. About seeing him again or about confessing her secret identity? She couldn't tell. She pushed the nervousness aside and opened her contract. She read it carefully. Satisfied by the offer she printed it. Signed it. Scanned it.

She opened her email and clicked reply.

Mr. Abraham,

Words escape me at the moment to fully express my gratitude. Please find attached a scanned copy of the signed contract.

I will look over the suggested changes and send you my revised manuscript and art selection by Friday as you have requested.

Again, thank you so much for believing in my work.

Sincerely,

MV

Before she lost her nerves she hit send and opened the art sketches. Her eyes watered at the bright colors provided in the first option. The beach scene of the setting sun with blazing oranges and mauves and pinks didn't sit well with her so she easily discarded this one. The next one provided a darker scene – stark naked beach – no signs of life for the exception of a half open door and soft pool of light. This one had potential. The third pulled at her heart strings, gentle waves rolled above a full moon, in its light the silhouette of a woman could be seen and in the darker shadows more silhouettes could be made out. The title of her book beautifully inscribed in gold dream dust with twinkles of it falling in the waves. Tears ran down her cheeks as her fingers traced the image on the screen.

She knew this would be the image that would represent her book.

The grandfather clock struck four. She saved the art and shut down her work station. She closed the lights and shut the door. In the kitchen she started preparing dinner.

***

Max pulled in to Myriam's drive way. His heart rate sped up at the thought of seeing her. Kissing her. Making love to her again, and again. He practically ran up her drive to ring the doorbell. The smile she gave him as she pulled him out of the cold into her warm embrace heated him through and through. Her lips found his and claimed them. His tongue danced with hers as she backed them out of the stoop. He kicked the door shut with the heel of his foot.

"You're so beautiful." He breathed when their kiss broke off.

She pulled at the sleeve of his jacket and helped him out of it. He bent down to unlace his boots and toed them off before following her in the kitchen.

"It smells good." He sniffed the spicy air appreciatively.

"It's not ready yet."

"When will it be?"

"In about an hour."

He grabbed her around the waist and twirled her in his arms.

"An hour." He breathed into her hair.

"Yes."

He squeezed her butt and dragged her across his stiff cock.

"Let me make love to you."

She molded herself to him and kissed him hard and deep. His hands reached the hem of her t-shirt. He pulled it up over her head and let it fall to the floor. She took his hand and guided him in the living room. His eyes ravished her luscious breasts bound in a deep purple satin bra. His breath hitched in his throat. She sat down and patted the cushion next to hers. He settled into it and found her lips waiting for his. His hands reached behind her back. Hook by hook he undid her bra. He moved his fingers up to her shoulders and glided the straps down. The cups fell off her breasts and they spilled into his waiting hands. She moaned in pleasure as he pressed her nipples against his palms.

"Max, I need to touch you." She breathed.

He pulled away and peeled off his shirt, pants and briefs.

"I am all yours," he whispered.

Her hands touched him everywhere. He leaned her further into the buttery couch and tugged down her yoga pants. The deep purple satin triangle called to him. He slowly traced the outer edges of it. Slipped his finger underneath the sexy garment and found her wet slit. He groaned appreciatively. He slid his finger out and brought it to his lips. She tasted sweet and tangy. Her mouth trailed sloppy open-mouthed kisses down his chest. She continued over his belly button and lower. Lower. *God, yes.* She sucked in his cock to the hilt. This time he wanted to fuck her mouth. He grabbed handfuls of hair on either side of her head and stopped her bobbing motion.

"Relax," he coaxed as he started pumping in and out her mouth, "breathe through your nose, love," he cooed and pumped faster in and out her lips scraping his bulging veins across her teeth. His hold in her hair tightened. He pushed his erection further in. Quickly pulled out and began thrusting in and out in rapid succession. "Myriam, this feels so good," he grunted as he continued to move in and out harder and deeper.

"Suck me, love," he begged as he relinquished control.

Her mouth moved slowly up. Slowly down. Tongue twirling around his girth. Twirl up. Twirl down. Suction – unbelievable suction – glued him to the roof her mouth and that sweet tongue of hers glided over his bulging veins. The suction subsided. The bobbing started and the tempo increased with every bob. Her hands cupped his rock hard balls squeezed them together. He came hard in the back her throat. He felt her swallow his white ribbons of desire.

"Christ, Myriam, you drive me crazy. The sight of you is enough to get me hard again." He crushed his lips to hers and tasted himself there.

His hands cupped her breasts, circling her erect nipples. His eyes burned with desire. "So beautiful," he murmured before he sucked one of the little pebbles in his mouth. She arched her back inviting him to take it deeper. He did. His hands moved down her body and pulled on her panties. They slid off without resistance. The smell of her arousal intoxicated him. His finger found her swollen clit and pinched it. Her hips bucked.

"Max, please," she said

He released her nipple and dropped his head between her legs. He flicked her nub and licked her glistening slit. He parted her pussy lips with his tongue and plunged it inside – still so unbelievably tight – her muscles constricted around the tip of his tongue and then quickly released it. He couldn't wait anymore. He lifted his head. Dragged his body over hers and plunged into her wet heat. Sanity left him. Her sweet, enveloping tightening heat brought him to edge. His mouth licked and bit any inch of exposed skin it found. His cock throbbed and pumped. His fingers pinched her clit harder.

"Max," she panted.

He spread her legs further apart and kept plunging in and out her swollen pussy lips – his finger rubbing, pinching, flicking her sensitive clit. Her hot wet walls tightened around him. In quick succeeding motion she squeezed his cock milking him to the last drop.

"Max! Max! Max!" She screamed his name as her pussy overflowed with their juices.

***

Synchronized coming must be an art for him, Myriam mused. She held him inside of her affectionately giving him little squeezes. He kissed her long and deep. Unable to keep his softening cock from slipping out her oozing pussy she let him pull out. He stood. Looked at her with that lopsided grin of his and headed out of the room. Her muscles didn't response when she tried to sit up and get off the couch. She felt utterly spent in the most delicious way. Max came back with a wash cloth. It felt cool against her over-hot skin as he cleaned her thighs and pussy. He quickly cleaned himself as well. They dressed just in time. The oven timer beeped.

Myriam served dinner. Max poured the wine.

The butterflies danced in her belly making her lose her appetite. She pushed her food around her plate. Max tucked in and enjoyed every bite of her chicken parmesan. He pushed his empty plate aside and looked at her with an arched brow.

"Is everything ok?"

Myriam knew she couldn't wait much longer he needed to know her secret.

"Myriam?"

She could tell her silence made him anxious.

"I received some news today and, and I-I-I,"

"What?"

His eyes clouded with worry and something much more potent. The naked fear she read there made her gulp. She twisted her hands until they turned white.

"I love you Myriam, nothing you say will change that."

She fervently hoped so. She turned around opened the top drawer of the island and pulled out the stapled contract. She took a deep breath, faced him and glided the contract on the table. For a long time he remained silent. Her heart sank as she watched his features turn to stone.

Cold.

Hard.

Impenetrable.
Stone.
Without a word.
Or a glance.
Not even a pause.
He walked out.

Myriam sank to the floor. Air left her lungs. Her blood turned to frosty slush in her veins. Her lips turned blue. Her fingers white. The tears sliding down her cheeks felt like ice.

A haunting scream filled her head.

***

Max walked and walked and walked. Oblivious the cold December air he kept on walking. His mind lost. How could it be? Why had she never told him? This could ruin him. The contract, *her* contract, would be annulled. His job – gone. With his mind in turmoil, his feet guided him. The soft sole of his shoes crunched on the snow and gravel of the path. The sound brought him back to the moment. His eyes snapped to the tombstone before him.

"I am lost, Juls," he cried and sank to his knees.

"She threw me off kilter, sis. Never. Ever. Could I have guessed this. Arthur will have my head." Max snorted out loud. "He can have it. She took my heart. Left a gaping hole in my chest in its stead. Why did she do this?"

The wind twirled round and round capturing him in a mini cyclone pressing against his frame. He fought against it. Tooth and nail he pushed at the unseen arms enfolding him.

"NO!"

The wind died.

A haunting scream filled his mind.

***

Myriam didn't know how long she stayed in her catatonic state. One moment the shattered jagged pieces of her entire being were ice, the next a serene force infused her core, mended the pieces together and coaxed life back into her limbs. She struggled to lift her frame from the floor. The uphill battle left her drained. She clutched the counter top and eased herself foot by painful foot towards the tower.

It's the only place they hadn't shared together. Somehow she made it up to the library. Her body convulsed from the effort and she collapsed in the buttery leather love seat.

"Juls, I know I am still alive, but I wonder how that's possible. I am numb all over. Frozen through and through how can my heart beat when I no longer feel the flow of blood coursing through me? How can I still have a voice when the air forms icicles in my lungs? How Juls? Why?"

***

Max made his way home in a daze. He climbed up the stairs to his condo. His eyes registered the For Sale sign affixed to his balcony... it didn't shake him enough to shock him out of his trance. He unlocked his door and walked in the dark entrance. He didn't bother switching on the lights. He simply kept on walking past the guest bathroom and up the stairs.

His mind in complete anguish with nothing he could do to be rid of it. Not rubbing his hands on his face and forehead or digging his fingers deep into his scalp. At some point sleep claimed him. His long frame tossed and turned. The sinuous limbs beaded with cold sweat beneath the sheets. The dark fingers of sleep kept him trapped in his own torment.

The sudden succession of shrill rings penetrated the darkness and brought him to awareness. Barely, and, the cacophony of rings kept on. His bleary eyes squinted as the light of the midday sun hit him in the face. The ear-splitting noise of the rings still echoing all around him made everything inside of him vibrate. Max picked up the receiver.

"Hello," he grunted in a rough whisper

"Mr. Abraham, is that you," Janine's perky voice asked.

"Yeah," he rasped

"Oh my, you must have caught the flu that's been going around," she sympathized. She gave him the perfect out.

"Huh-huh."

"Don't you worry Mr. Abraham I'll re-schedule your meetings. I'll send you and Mr. Blooms the updated calendar by the end of day," she promised.

"Thanks Janine," he whispered.

After he placed the phone back in its cradle Max had the presence of mind to pick-up his blackberry and set his out of office reply on his email. Once done he threw the cell on the chair across the room and the dark fingers of sleep claimed him once again.

***

Days passed, but Myriam didn't see them. Everything blurred together. She remained curled on the buttery leather love seat. Dammit! Why couldn't this be the year of the such dreaded apocalypse? If the end of the world would come in flames of fire or shard of ice she'd welcomed it. Heck, maybe the Mayans got their calculation wrongs and this would the year that will do us all in. Here's hoping!! Alas, no. The days dragged on by.

***

The loud boom of a fist rattling his front door seemed to shake the entire frame of the house. Max bolted upright in his bed. The insistent knocking came again; louder this time. He got up. Briskly ran his hands down his rumpled clothes. Persistent the woody rattle shook the rafters once more. He flew down the steps and tore the front door open.

"Arthrur?" His mouth felt pasty from lack of use.

"Max," the older man said and arched a brow.

Max moved aside and let him in.

Arthur pushed his large frame inside the vestibule, doffed off his lamb skin jacket and leather gloves. He turned to stare at the man he considered to be one of his best agents. Max cringed under the scrutiny the older man bore him. He knew he looked liked shit – rumpled clothes, bleary red eyes; hair going whichever way, days worth of subtle covered his chin and jaw. He wanted to make apologies for his sorry appearance. He didn't have too.

"I taught so," the old man smirked "it's more than the flu keeping you abed. Go clean yourself up. We'll talk after."

Max heard the dismissal in his tone and flew back up the stairs. He peeled the clothes from his body and jumped in the shower. Dressed in pair of clean jeans and a long sleeve T Max padded back down the stairs. He found Arthur in his small study.

"You wanted to talk?"

"Have a seat Max."

Max sank into his favorite chair and waited.

"When Janine told me last week you had the flu I thought nothing of it. *At first*. Then I got to thinking."

Max's mind reeled. Last week. Had a week already passed? His total lack of comprehension must have shown on his face because Arthur confirmed the date when he stated "Max, it's Christmas Eve."

Arthur paused to let that sink in.

"Anyways, seeing as I'll be going on vacation I wanted to come by and finalize this contract with you."

Pain seared him.

"I must say I really did enjoy Miss Valentine's novel."

The gaping hole in his chest pulsed.

"Or should I say Miss Volterre."

Max's jaw dropped.

"I thought so."

"Arthur, I didn't know. I swear."

"I know."

Confusion clearly showed on his features, though he felt glad that somehow the rage simmering in his belly didn't became evident to the older man – his mentor.

"What?"

"Max, when this manuscript," Arthur said pulling out the piece from his briefcase and brandying it about "first came in to Blooms the address label clearly stipulated for the package to be delivered to Darla. In her cover letter Miss Volterre explained her wish of the use of her pseudonym, total honesty and forthcoming in her relationship with you she politely stated that our policies, as so advertised, did not specify that she couldn't submit her work to another agent with whom she did not interact on "friendly" terms with and she did request that you not be informed of this submission. Darla came to me with the bundle..."

"...And you decided to fuck up my life by sending it down to me. Arthur, when Myriam showed me the contract I'd sent *Miss Valentine*," the name came out of his lips in a sneer "I – Oh dear God – I," blood drained from his face.

"I am sorry Max; I never meant to make you think you'd infringed upon company policy. I hoped to speak with you before your friend disclosed her..." seeing how distraught the younger man acted Arthur could only deduce that his first impressions were correct "you love her, she loves you. GO. Now. This the season for miracles."

Max darted out of his chair and out the door before Arthur had a chance to move.

***

Myriam watched the snow fall.

Big fluffy flakes danced on the wings of the wind.

Hypnotised by the swirling and twirling she never heard the doorbell. Nor the front door being opened and closed. Or the footsteps in the hall and on the stairs. Entranced she felt numb. Her body hollow. An empty shell really. Her essence followed *him*. White-hot pokers of pain pierced her numbness. She clutched her torso in a hard hug pressing her arms tight against her chest to stop the pain from seeping out – useless attempt.

The haunting scream that had been echoing in her mind for days tore out of her.

Gentle arms wrapped around her.

"Hush, sweetheart, hush" a soft voice cooed.

WAIT. NOT JUST A VOICE. HIS VOICE. MAX'S VOICE. Her subconscious screamed at her. Her throat clogged up. The haunting scream died.

"Myriam, please look at me," he pleaded.

She lifted her head, but kept her eyes cast down; she didn't want to give him the pleasure of seeing them rimmed-red from frozen tears.

"I am sorry," his pain-filled voice broke her resolve.

Myriam lifter her eyes and locked on his bleary ones searching them.

"I. Am. Sorry."

The honesty of each word burned in his eyes.

"I should've told you," she whispered.

"Myriam, I am the one that acted like a first class jerk so don't you dare try to take this on you." His nostrils flared with anger. "I walked out; on you. I didn't let you explain. I just left. Do you have any idea what that did to me? It nearly killed me. It tore out my heart knowing that I... I could do that..." he shook his head cursing his un-gibed tongue "I mean my leaving that night hurt you. I hurt you. I never meant to do that." Tears filled his blurry eyes and splashed down his cheeks.

Myriam's insides melted. She brought her trembling fingers to his face and brushed away his tears.

"Max, I really should have told you..." Her voice faltered, she sniffed back tears and gulp the lump that formed in her throat "...shame stood in my way."

"Ashamed!" The astonishment he felt rang clear in his voice, his features.

"Yes dammit! Is it so hard to believe that I felt ashamed? Come on, how could I not be? It's unheard of a woman like me – thirty-two years old virgin, pinning away for my best friend, writing erotic romance to curb an insatiable hunger that consumed me night and day. I knew I couldn't submit my work to you. I read Blooms "family and friends" policy very, very, carefully. I even stated a portion of it in my cover letter. I never lied to them... *only to you*." The last confession came out in a whisper.

"Myriam, Darla read the manuscript and recommended the publication of it to Arthur. He, for some reasons known only to him and God, decided to send it back down for a "2nd" reading – by me. You're a talented writer. Your words came to life. In vivid images. Raw emotions. Your Voice is exquisite. Don't be ashamed. Your book will rock the market."

Myriam blushed under his praises. She wanted him to hold her. Or maybe she wanted to hold him. All she knew is that she wanted to feel his arms around her. She wanted to feel his mouth on hers. She wanted his hands to glide over her contours and curves. She needed to feel his cock possess her pussy. She felt the moisture pool between her thighs. In a breathless voice she asked "Max," she stammered, her heart slammed against her rib cage afraid of rejection and even more afraid of losing him forever, she gulped and spoke with her heart "make love to me."

***

Blood rushed in his ears. His heart swelled. He'd been afraid he'd lost her and to his complete amazement she asked him what he so desperately wanted – to make love to her. In a half a heart beat his head bent down to hers.

"I am so sorry. I love you." He breathed before his mouth covered hers. His tongue plunged in her velvet mouth savoring the nectar hidden there. His fingers wrapped themselves in her thick auburn tresses. He titled her head back. Deepen the kiss. She moaned in his mouth. He groaned in response and broke off the kiss.

His mouth moved down the lovely column of her throat. His fingers released the silken strands and moved down her back. Pulling her closer to him. She molded herself to his frame. A perfect fit. He removed his clothes and undressed her. Relishing every new inch of skin exposed. Kissing a shoulder. Nibbling a nipple. Licking her belly button. Flicking her swollen clit. He loved watching the building arousal change her eyes. Dark. Stormy. Gray. His mouth moved back up and claimed hers in a kiss. His hands kept worshiping her hour glass figure. His fingers grazed her moist pussy lips. Her head arched back. She moaned from deep inside her throat as he slipped his finger inside.

Amazing still so fucking tight. He stroked her clit with his thumb. Her eyes smoldered. He lowered her onto the area rug. His mouth moved down her throat. Laved her breast with kisses and nibbles. Teased her belly button. Buried itself inside her sopping wet pussy lips. He licked and slurped up her delicate cream. Then it moved downwards her inner thigh. Licked her calf and sucked in her big toe. He released it with pop. His hands ever so gently pushed her thighs further apart. He moved in between her spread legs. Inch by inch he slipped his cock inside her molten core.

He took his time. Delighting in the feel of her tight walls as he slid slowly in, slowly out, her pussy felt like a skin tight glove made especially for him. He lowered his head to hers claimed her lips in a kiss. His hands caressed her breasts, teased her nipples. His cock languorously moved within her wet heat. She transported him to Heaven with her hot, wet, tight pussy and her trembling responses to his touches – her complete surrender of her body to him.

Never before had he had such an expressive lover. He enjoyed pleasing her. Sucking her beaded nipples. Kissing her lips. Circling her clit with his fingers. Filling her melting core. Stretching her pussy. Her hips undulated under him. Her nails created grooves in his back. He kept his slow amorous pace; depositing tender kisses on her nose, her eyelids, her throat, her clavicles, the swell of her breasts. His fingers circled and circled her pulsating clit. Her hips push up and out taking him deeper inside. Her back bowed off the floor. Her breathing grew heavy. So did his. He felt the blood rush in his veins. His cockhead expanded. He pinched her clit. She cried out. They exploded together.

"I love you, Max."

She gave his softening cock an affectionate squeeze before he pulled out and rolled off of her. He settled himself on the area rug and cuddled close to her.

The grand-father clock chimed. One. Two. Three. Four. Five. Six. Seven. Eight. Nine. Ten. Elven. Twelve.

"Merry Christmas, Myriam."

"Christmas?"

He chuckled at her questioning tone remembering that he too had not seen the days they spent apart go by and therefore had been taken aback when Arthur had announced it to be Christmas Eve.

"I have a present for you." The words were out of his mouth before he could stop them. Why did say that? He hadn't shopped. He had nothing to offer her. Yet, an overwhelming feeling came over him to pick up his jeans. When he did, he felt something in the side pocket. His fingers dipped in.

Impossible.

No other word could encompass the significance of it. Impossible. He knew without a doubt that Julianna had been buried with... how could this happen? He stopped questioning and simply sent a quick prayer to his twin and put the delicate band in the palm of his hand.

"Close your eyes," he asked softly and took her hands in his "I love you Myriam," the words came out with such fierceness as he let the band slip from his hand into hers.

***

Myriam eyes flew open.

Unconceivable.

Emotions choked her up. Tears blurred her eyes. Here lay the proof she so desperately needed. Her fingers tenderly traced the small band – the intricate knotting and twisting so familiar to her; Julianna's Celtic band – the one she wore one her finger before the casket closed over her. She brushed the tears away and searched Max's face for the meaning of this offering. His eyes shone with love, devotion, passion, hunger, and a promise of forever.

"Yes," she whispered before her lips captured his in a searing kiss.

Epilogue

December 17, 2014

Juls,
I can't breathe. The butterflies are suffocating me. No air is coming in, no matter how hard I try to pull and pull some in. I should be on cloud nine today, but...

I miss you like crazy
xxoxoox.

Myriam closed her journal and left it on her bed. The time had finally come.

***

Max ran a hand in his unruly burnt copper hair. No matter how much he tried to put the damn strands in place they just went this way and that. Giving up he let his hand drop to his side. When he looked up he saw her; she knocked his breath way. Her white velvet gown with deep lavender trimming accentuated all of her silhouette, before him stood the true definition of grace and beauty. She made her way towards him in slow, sure steps. He held out his hands to her as she approached and took his fingers and stood by his side.

Their priest, Father Thomas, looked at them and asked. "Are you sure you wish to be married here?"

Max understood why Father Thomas asked, after all, it's not every day a couple decides to get married in a cemetery. Knowing full well that nowhere else in the world would be more appropriate than right here for himself, or Myriam for that matter, he felt confident in his answer when he replied "We're sure."

Family and friends began trickling in and gathered around the grave.

***

Up in the clouds a young woman with burnt cooper hair as wild and unruly as the man below and sparkling hazel eyes danced with glee.

Took them long enough... I felt sure I would have to haunt them forever... Shudder the thought!

Acknowledgments

So much blood, sweat and tears, and, to this I add ink went into making this dream of mine come true. Sometimes I still can't believe this is happening. It wouldn't be happening without the fantastic support from my readers and publisher: House of Erotica. Thank you for believing in my work.

I can't pass up the opportunity to give a special acknowledgment to the original PoD ladies: Courtney, Hazel, Judy and Stephanie you have been my constant pillars over the years. Your unfailing support helped me find my voice; gave me wings. Thank you just doesn't seem to be enough. So I say, let's celebrate PoD style.

Once again thank you to my family – we are one crazy bunch – and I love it because in all our chaos the one constant rule applies: never give up! When I came close to calling it quits (more than once), I could always count one of you to bring me back up again to my writing board.

To my husband and girls I won't make promises I can't keep. I know you love my neurotic typing anyway...so when disappear inside my bubble again I know you will be there cheering me on. I can't express in words how much that means to me. All I can give you is all my love and affection when my feet hit the ground.

Last but not least I cannot forget my beta readers for helping me take this collection from frumpy to something spectacular with all their suggestions and edits and proof reading: Emily Susan and Jeff you've made this baby shine!

CPSIA information can be obtained at www.ICGtesting.com
Printed in the USA
LVOW07s1928010615

440756LV00001B/25/P

9 781785 380600